Jami

The Behâristân

Abode of Spring

Jami

The Behâristân
Abode of Spring

ISBN/EAN: 9783337367466

Printed in Europe, USA, Canada, Australia, Japan

Cover: Foto ©Andreas Hilbeck / pixelio.de

More available books at **www.hansebooks.com**

THE BEHÂRISTÂN

BY

JÂMI

THE BEHÂRISTÂN

(ABODE OF SPRING)

BY

JÂMI

A LITERAL TRANSLATION FROM THE PERSIAN

Printed by the Kama Shastra Society for Private Subscribers only

---

𝔅𝔢𝔫𝔞𝔯𝔢𝔰

1887

CONTENTS.

INTRODUCTION.

SA'DI's Gulistan, or Rose Garden, (finished A.D. 1258) is a work well known in Europe, but by expurgated editions only. It was followed in A.D. 1334 by a work of the same nature, entitled The Nigaristan, or. Picture Gallery, by Mu'in-uddin Jawini, which has not yet been translated into any European language. And this, again, was followed by a similar work in A.D. 1487, called The Behâristân, or Abode of Spring, by the great Persian poet Nur-uddin Abdur Rahman, otherwise known as Jâmi.

The Kama Shastra Society now proposes to issue un-expurgated translations of the three books above mentioned. The series will be found to be useful and interesting, both to the man of the world, and to the Oriental student, neither of whom can acquire a true knowledge of men and things without a study of the realities. To them then a mutilated work is not half so useful as a book containing the whole writings of any author, whose effusions are really worth perusing.

At the same time it must be stated that in this Behâristân, or Abode of Spring,—the translation of which will appear in the following pages,—there is really very little indeed to be objected to. A few remarks or stories scattered here and there would have to be omitted in an edition printed for public use, or for public sale. But on the whole the author breathes the noblest and purest sentiments, and illustrates his meanings by the most pleasing, respectable, and apposite tales, along with numerous extracts from the Qurân.

About the poet Jâmi himself a few words are necessary. He has been generally called the last great poet and mystic of Persia, and is said to have combined the moral tone of Sa'di with the lofty aspirations of Jalal-uddin Rumi ; the graceful ease of Hafiz with the deep pathos of Nizami. He devoted his whole life to literature, and was endowed with such extensive learning that he was supposed to be a complete master of the Persian language, in which he was certainly one of the most gifted and productive of writers. He was the author of many works, not only in poetry, but also in prose. The total number is said to amount to forty-five or fifty.

Jâmi was born in A.D. 1414, at Jam, a small town not far from Hirât, the capital of Khorâsân ; and from his native place he took his *nom de plume*, or *nom du poète*, of Jâmi, which means also a drinking cup as well as a native of Jam. He died at Hirât in A.D. 1492, mourned by the whole city.

TRANSLATOR'S PREFACE.

THE Behâristân, or Abode of Spring, is divided into eight chapters, called gardens, which, the author states, he had composed, in the first instance, for the instruction of his own son. The beginning is written entirely in the style of the mysticism of the Sûfis, and from it some slight ideas may be gathered about their tenets; gradually, however, anecdotes are introduced on a variety of subjects, but in the third garden they are mostly about kings, and some of these are excellent. The fourth garden deals with the praises of liberality, embodied in little stories, several of which appear to be founded on actual events, like those of the preceding chapter, and may also, on that score, be considered interesting. The fifth garden is entirely on love affairs, from which something may be learned of the customs and opinions in vogue among the people concerning such matters, and there is scarcely anything which will greatly shock the taste of European readers. The sixth garden has been already done into English by Mr. C. G. Wilson, under the title of " Persian Wit and Humour." It is the only chapter of the work that has as yet appeared in English in any shape, but is not so fully or so faithfully rendered as the present trans-

B

lation.   The seventh garden may be called a brief anthology
of thirty-five poets, containing specimens of their compositions, and will, perhaps, be one of the most pleasing portions
of this little book, but the eighth, or last garden, has also
its attractions, and consists entirely of animal fables, twenty-
three in number.   It is hoped that the 175 foot-notes
appended to this translation will prove acceptable.

THE BEHÂRISTÂN

[ABODE OF SPRING]

OF JÂMI,

IN THE NAME OF ALLAH, THE MERCIFUL, THE CLEMENT!

———

Verses :

When a bird intent to soar aloft, from the beginning
Fails to invoke the strength of Praise and flies,
It sheds its plumage ere it attains its purpose,
And falls to rise no more.

Many thousand hymns of praise are warbled by the birds
of the vernal abode of love and fidelity, from the leafy pul-
pits of virtue and beneficence, in beautiful voices and
harmonious melodies to the end of all time, which are by
the auditory organs of holy congregations and the superin-
tendents of human affairs perpetually conveyed :—

Verses :

To the Maker—the rose grove of the sphere
Is but one leaf of the flower-garden of His creation—

B 2

That those who sing His praises

May have a plate of pearls and jewels full of oblations.
May the magnitude of His glory shine, and the word of His
perfection be exalted !

A thousand chants of salutation and greeting from the
philomels of the garden-mansion of *union* and benevolence,
who are the musicians of the assembly of witnesses and
songsters in the delightful house of *extacy* and benevolence.*

Verses :

To the *paragon* of the garden of eloquence—of which
The rose of this grove is but one leaf,
The birds take from the leaves of the meadow
Nothing but a lesson of the qualities of His beauty—
and to his companions and family who have participated in
the radiations of his knowledge and his vicinity† :

But after [this preamble the author says]:—As at present
my darling and beloved son Ziâ-uddin-Yusuf—may Allah
preserve him from what will bring grief and affliction upon
me—is engaged in studying the rudiments of the Arabic
language, and acquiring various other branches of a liberal

---

* *Union* is the 7th and *extacy*, the 5th degree, or stage, of a Sufi's
journey to perfection.

† The *paragon* is the prophet to whom and to whose connections
praise is given, but the sense of this whole preamble may be considered
simply to mean that praises are first due to Allah and then to the
prophet.

education ; and as it is well-known that young boys and inexperienced youths become very disheartened and un-happy when they receive instruction in idiomatic expressions they were not accustomed to, and never heard of, I made him now and then read a few lines from the *Gulistân* of that celebrated Sheikh and great master, Muslihuddin S'adi Shirâzi.

Verses:

Nine *Gulistans*,* a garden of paradise,
The very brambles and rubbish of which are of the nature of ambergris
The gates are the doors to paradiset
The abundant stories are so many *Kawthers*‡
The sallies of wit by curtains hidden
Are the envy of the *Hûris*§ brought up delicately;
The poems as lofty trees are delightful
From the pleasant dew of *the rivers below them.*‖

On that occasion it occurred to me to compose a tract in imitation of that noble prose and poetry, that those who

---

* The Gulistan has only 8 chapters, but here 9 are mentioned, which will be true if its preface be also counted as one.

† The word *Bâb* means *gate* and also *chapter*, like the Latin *caput* which means *head*.

‡ *Kawther* is one of the rivers of paradise.

§ *Hûris* are the immaculate virgins of paradise.

‖ This expression is in Arabic *tahtihâ-allânhâr*, and stands here as a figure of speech to designate *paradise*, in connection with which it occurs several times in the Qurân.

are present may hear, and the absent may read it. Having accomplished this purpose :—

Verses :

I asked intellect how I am to adorn this fresh bride
So that her attractions may be enchanced to those who court
  her ;
It replied :—Scatter pearls of laudation to the ruling sove-
  reign,
The aid of the world, honour of the religion, refuge of the
  west and east,
Star of the constellation of glory, jewel of the casket of nobility
Lamp of the assembly and beloved of Timûr Khân Sultân
  Hasan,
Who is powerful like the heaven, and sun of the earthly
  atoms of the world,
To be looked upon with favour by him, is the sum of hap-
  piness,
He is religious and relieves by his liberality all the necessi-
  ties of the people,
His generosity disapproves of the shame of indebtedness.
May Allah, the Most High, favour his partizans, augment
his power and perpetuate his noble progeny under the
shadow of his country and government, and make all his
subjects contented under the wings of his justice and beneficence.

Verses :

Though ere this the Gulistân was by S'adi
Completed in the name of S'ad Ben Zanki

My Behâristân takes its name from him
Whose slave S'ad Ben Zanki might perhaps be.

Verses :

Take a walk in this Behâristân [abode of spring]
That you may see therein Gulistâns [rose groves]
With gracefulness in each Gulistân
Flowers growing and aromatic plants blooming.

This Behâristân is divided into eight gardens, each of which contains as many sub-divisions, with anemons of different colours and aromatic plants of various odours. Autumnal blasts cannot wither the anemons, nor frosts congeal the aromatic herbs.

Verses :

Its meadow grows around the sides
Its tulip beds bloom in the environs ;
The eartips of the tulips bear the perspiration of the dew,
By rain the cups of the buds are filled
" Precious are the tears from the eyes of anemons "
" Plentiful the laughter from the teeth of the anthemis."*
The wine-bibbing narcissus is beckoning
" Pardon my Transgression and I shall live."†
I fear that the graceful beckoning
Gives permission to abstainers.

It is requested that the promenaders in these gardens—

---

* The two lines with signs of quotation are in Arabic.
† Likewise in Arabic.

which contains no Thorns intended to give offence, nor rubbish displayed for interested purposes—walking through them with sympathetic steps and looking at them carefully, will bestow their good wishes, and rejoice with praise the gardener who has spent much trouble and made great exertions in planning and cultivating these gardens.

Verses :

I.et every fortunate man who of these blooming trees
The shade enjoys, or the fruit consumes
Act according to the laws of righteousness,
Walk on the road of generosity and pray thus :—
May *Jámi*, who planted this garden O Lord
Be always full of God and empty of self.*
May he travel on no other path but His, and seek no other
    union† but His,
Nor utter another name but His, nor see another face but
    His.

---

* The meaning of *Jámi*, the author's name, is *a goblet*, hence the play of the words full and empty.

† Union is the seventh degree of the Sûfis, as has already been remarked.

FIRST GARDEN

*Exhibition of aromatic herbs, culled from the gardens of
those who have seen far on the road of right direction,
and who occupy the chief seats in the pavilion
of excellency.*

Junaid, the prince of the tribe (may his secret be sanctified) has said that the words of Sheikhs skilled in science
and *knowledge** are an army of the armies of God the Most
High in the mansion of every heart, by means of which the
intentions of the enemies, passion and lust, are put to flight.

Verses :

When passion and lust, which are combatants for Satan
Assail the heart of a God-fearing man
Only the armies of maxims of directors
By their power defeat those highway robbers.

God the Most High has said to His prophet (the benediction of Allah be upon him and peace) :—" We shall narrate
to thee histories of apostles by which we shall confirm thy
heart.")†

---

* The fourth degree or stage ; the word is *m'arifat.*
† Qurân, ch. XI., v. 121.

Verses :
When you shape in your heart a figure by your will
You must impart life to it from the breath blown in the
    Trumpet of ' *Arifs* '*
And if your heart becomes fluttering from emotions of nature
Inflame it with explanations from the stories of pious men.

The *Pir*,† may his secret be sanctified, enjoined his fol-
lowers to remember the sayings of every Pir, and if they are
not able, to keep in mind at least their names in order to
profit by them.

Verses :
O you from whose name love is raining
From whose book and message love is flowing
Every one who passes near your door becomes a *lover*‡
Yea from your door and roof love is pouring.

There is a tradition that on the morn of resurrection God
the Most High will ask a poor and destitute worshipper :—
" Hast thou known such and such a scholar or 'Arif in such
a place ? " and he will reply :—" Yes, I knew him." Then
the command will arrive : — " I have given him to
thee."

---

* *'Arif* is in common language simply a man who knows ; an intelligent person ; but among Sûfis an individual who has attained high
spiritual knowledge.

† In the ordinary sense *Pir* is an old man, but in religion *a spiritual
director*.

‡ The word lover, *'Adsheg* means in the Sûfi idiom *lover of God;* he
is a man who has made progress in spiritual life like the *'Arif*.

Verses :

My dignity in the ranks of thy lovers is higher
Than that I should covet the various stages of union.
On my heart the name of mendicant at Thy door is printed ;
The seal of reception is a sufficient record of deeds for me.

STORY.

Seri Sagti (may his secret be sanctified) gave to Junaid
some work to do, which he performed satisfactorily ; whereon
the former threw to him a paper with the following inscrip
tion on it :—

Arabic Verses.

A camel driver running in the desert said,
I weep, and who will tell thee why I weep?
I weep for fear that thou wilt leave me,
Wilt sever my ties and wilt exile me.

Verses :

I weep blood, how should I conceal it from thee,
Wherefore I keep these two eyes weeping,
Although I have a heart rejoiced by union
I have a hundred wounds on it for fear of separation.

Junaid (m. h. s. b. s.) also says :—" One day I entered the
house of Seri, whereon he recited the following distich."—

Arabic Verses :

There is no pleasure in the day, and none in the night,
I care not whether the night be lenghtened or shortened.

STORY.

Hulláj having been asked who is a disciple, said :—" He,

who from the beginning makes the Lord God his aim, is pacified by nothing, and associates with no man till he reaches Him."

Verses :

For Thee we have hastened across land and sea
Have passed over plains, and mountains climbed,
Have turned away from whatever we met
Until we found the way to the sanctuary of union with Thee.

STORY.

Abu Hâshem the Sûfi (m. h. s. b. s.) has said :—" It is easier to dig up a mountain from the root with the point of a needle, than to eradicate the baseness of pride from the heart :—

Verses :

Boast not of having no pride, because it is more invisible
Than the mark of an ant's foot on a black rock in a dark
     night ;
Think it not easy to extirpate it from thy heart
For, it is more easy to root up a mountain from the earth
     with a needle."

STORY.

Zul-Nun*—m. h. s. b. s.—went for purposes of enquiry to one of the West African Sheikhs, who said to him :—" What hast thou come for? If thou hast come to learn the science

---

* This is the name of a prophet mentioned also in the Qurân. He is believed to be the same with the Biblical Jonah.

of the ancients and the moderns, there is no possibility; the creator knows it all; and if thou hast come to seek Him, He was there, where thou hast made thy first step."

Verses:

Ere this I possessed Thee not externally of me
In my abundant travels I had hoped to find Thee
Now that I found Thee, I know that Thou art He
Whom I had abandoned at my first step.

STORY.

The Pir of Hirât says :—" He accompanies His seeker, and having taken hold of his hand, hastens in search of Himself."

Verses:

He, neither whose name nor whose sign I know
Is after taking my hand dragging me after Himself.
He is my hand as well as my foot, wherever He goes,
I advance dancing and clapping my hands.

STORY.

Fyzal 'Ayâz (m. h. s. b. s.) says :—" I worship God (who be praised and exalted) from friendship ; because I cannot help worshipping Him." Some of his companions asked him :—" Who is base ?" He replied :—" He who adores God from fear and hope." They further asked :—" Then how dost thou worship Him ?" He replied :—" With love; and His friendship keeps me in service and obedience."

Verses:

When will the burning [agony] of him who is the victim of
love be under the dark ground ?

Since this fire has been kindled by His luminous soul
How can the lover withdraw his head from the collar of
  obedience,
As on a ringdove His collar has grown upon his neck.

Verses :

Beloved ! I cannot be far from Thy door
Cannot be satisfied with paradise and with Hûris.
My head is on Thy threshold by love's command, not for
  wages
Whatever I may do, I cannot bear to be away from this door·

STORY.

M'arif Kurkhi (m. h. s. b. s.) has said :—" The Sûfi is a
guest here ; it is a molestation that the guest should exact
anything from the host; because a guest hopes only for
politeness and claims nothing."

Verses :

I am Thy guest in the line of the willing*
I wait and am contented with whatever comes from Thee
Placing the eye of hope upon the table of Thy generosity
Hoping for Thy favours and not exacting them.

STORY.

Bayazid having been asked what the *traditional* and the
divine law amounted to, he replied, that the former is to
abandon the world, and the latter to associate with the
Lord.†

---

* Namely those willing and desiring intimacy with God.
† These two laws are the *Sonna* and the *Farz*.

Verses :

O thou who concerning the law of the men of the period
Askest about the traditional and divine command ;
The first is to turn the soul from the world away
The second is to find the way of proximity to the Lord.

STORY.

Shibli (m. h. s. b. s.) having become demented was taken
to the hospital and visited by acquaintances. He asked
who they were, and they replied :—" Thy friends," whereon
he took up a stone and assaulted them. They all began to
run away, but he exclaimed :— " O pretenders, return.
Friends do not flee from friends, and do not avoid the stones
of their violence."

Verses :

He is a friend, who although meeting with enmity
From his friend, only becomes more attached to him.
If he strikes him with a thousand stones of violence
The edifice of his love will only be made more firm by them.

It is also narrated of him, that when he once fell sick,
the Khalifah sent a Christian physician to treat him, who
asked him :—" What does thy mind crave for ? " He
replied :—" That thou shouldst become a Musalmân." The
doctor asked :—" Wilt thou get well and arise from the
couch of sickness if I become a Musalmân ?" The patient
having replied in the affirmative, and thereon induced the
the physician to make his possession of the Faith, he immediately got up from his bed, his malady disappeared and
left no trace. Accordingly both went to the Khalifah and

narrated their case. The Khalifah then said :—" I imagined I had sent a physician to a sick man, but now I find that the contrary was the case."

Verses :

Who has fallen sick from an attack of love
Knows that to meet his beloved is to meet his physician.
If the doctor from paradise places the foot on his head
He cures the physician from the disease of intoxication.

STORY.

Sohl 'Abdullah Justari (m. h. s. b. s.) says :—" Have nothing to do with a man who thinks in the morning what he is going to eat."

Verses :

Who rises in the morning from sleep with no other thoughts
Except ideas about food ; look for no sagacity in him,
He no sooner uncovers his feet, and raises his head from
    the pillow
Than he stretches his hand to the table. Wash thy hands
    of him.

STORY.

Abu S'ayd Khurrâz (m. h. s. b. s.) says :— " At the commencement of my state of willingness* I was guarding the secret of my time† and went one day into the desert. Whilst walking I heard in my rear a voice of something, but

---

* This was alluded to already in note on page 14.
† The locution is obscure to me. It appears to mean that he kept his mind concentrated.

restrained my heart from feeling and my eyes from looking. It approached me however, and when it had come near I preceived that two big lions had mounted on my back. I looked at them and said nothing when they mounted nor when they alighted."

Verses :

Who is the Sûfi, void of the intention of severance ?

He who turns his face to one colour, in this mansion of two colours,

He who does not sever the bond of his secret from the Beloved, even if

His path is beset by a wolf on one side, and a tiger on the other.

He has also said :—" Whoever imagines that *union** may be attained by great exertion, has taken trouble in vain, and whoever thinks that it may be reached without effort has travelled merely on the road of desire, because not everyone who ran took the *Gôr*, but he took the *Gôr* who ran [wisely].†

Verses :

By labour no one has reached the treasure of union.

It is strange that without labour no one has seen a treasure

Not every one who ran has captured the *Gôr*

But he captured the *Gôr-i-Khar* who ran [wisely].

---

* Union with God, mentioned in footnote p. 4.

† The word *Gôr* means onager, and also tomb, but even the word *Khar*, ass, appended to the versified piece which follows does not make the meaning clear, and I have tried to do so by adding the word wisely in brackets.

C

STORY.

Abu Bakar of Wasit (m. h. s. b. s.) says :—" Who alleges that he is near [to God] is far ; and who alleges that he is distant, is by his annihilation veiled in His [God's] existence."*

Verses :

Whoever says, I am near to that soul of the world
His pretence of nearness is, because he is distant,
And who says, I am far from Him; that distance of his
Is concealment within the veil of His proximity.

STORY.

Abu-l-Hasan of Qawsaj (m. h. s. b. s.) says :—" In the world there is nothing more disagreeable than a friend from interested motives or for retribution."

Verses :

A lover who expects a gift for separation from the Friend
Or desires attendance at the door of His union
Has no equal in baseness in the world
Because he has a desire besides the friendship of the Friend.

STORY.

Abu 'Ali Daqâq (m. h. s. b. s.) says that in the latter portion of his life he was so overcome with longing† that he mounted daily to the top of his house, turned towards the sun, and addressed to it the words :—" O wanderer over

---

* This is analogous to the *Nirvâna* of the Hindus.

† The word used in the text is *pain*, but I rendered it by *longing* which better expresses the Sûfi's desire for union with God.

the country! As thou hast been and art passing to-day, hast thou anywhere met any one afflicted like me, and hast thou anywhere obtained information of those who are utterly perplexed by this state?" and continued in this strain till sunset.

Verses :

O sun! There is no traveller in the world like Thee
Hast thou not brought me any gift from this journey?
Whom hast thou seen this day, who on the path of love
Showed life on his brow* and felt pain in his heart?

STORY.

Sheikh Abu-l-Hasan Khurqâni (m. h. s. b. s.) one day asked his companions what the best thing is? They replied: "Do, tell it thyself." Whereon he said :—"The heart which at all times keeps up the remembrance of the Friend."†

Verses:

I possess a little heart, which in all the feelings it enjoyed
Recorded on the tablets of the mind, the remembrance of
no one but Thee.
The remembrance of Thee has so filled it, that within it
No room is left for anything but Thee.

STORY.

Sheikh Abu S'aid Abu-l-Khair (m. h. s. b. s.) having been

---

* Or, literally *who had dust on his cheek ;* but this expression would be rather awkward in English.

† The words *Friend, Beloved,* &c., with a capital initial always stand for *God.*

asked what Sûfism is, replied :—" What thou hast in thy head, thou must put away, what thou hast in the hand, thou must give away, and thou must not lose thy temper, let happen what may."

Verses :

If thou desirest to get rid of self by becoming a Sûfi
Thou must purge thy head of lust and passion ;
Put away from thy hand whatever thou hast in it
And suffer a hundred wounds undismayed.

STORY.

The same Sheikh also said :—" It is magnanimous to pardon thy brothers when they offend thee, and so to deal with them that thou mayest never be required to ask their pardon."

Verses :

Magnanimity consists in two things O noble fellow,
Let me tell thee, and hearken that I may do so well :—
The first is, to forgive thy companions
If thou seest a hundred defects in one moment.
The second that thou at no time commit
A deed for which thou must their pardon crave.

STORY.

Bashar Hâfi (may Allah have mercy on him) having been asked by a disciple with what kind of a relish he ought to eat bread when he obtained some, replied :—" Remember the blessing of health, and consider it as thy relish."

Verses :

When a needy man places dry bread before himself
To nourish the spirit from the table of poverty,*
And his natural appetite then craves for a relish,
There is none better than the consciousness of health.

STORY.

Shaqiq Balkhi (m. h. s. b. s.) has said :—" Abstain from
associating with a rich man, because when thy heart becomes
attached to him, and thou hast been gladdened by his
liberality, thou hast taken another protector besides God
the Most High."

Verses :

When thou encounterest a wealthy man
Join him not for the sake of a livelihood,
Consider not a miser as thy surety
Take not a ruler for thy God.

STORY.

Yùsuf Abu-l-Hasan (m. h. s. b. s.) has said :—" All good
things are in a house, the key of which is humility and low-
liness." Also :—" All bad things are in a house, the key to
which is wealth and desire."

Verses :

All benefits are in one house, and there is
No other key to it except humility

---

* Ascetics generally believe that meagre and poor diet nourishes the
spiritual and deadens the carnal faculties of man ; the Romans had
already said :—*Sine Baccho et Cerere friget Venus.*

Thus also, all evils are connected in one house
Which has no other key but wealth and wishes.

STORY.

Sammûn Muhabb (m. h. s. b. s.) has said :—" A worshipper will never realise the pure love of the Lord, unless he
despises the whole world."

Verses :

If love of Eternal Beauty has taken root in thy heart
Thou wilt never lift the eyes of hope towards the Hûris of
    paradise.
How can Eternal Love be granted to thee
Unless thou accuse the whole universe of turpitude.

STORY.

Abu Bakar Warrâq (m. h. s. b. s.) has said :—"When
covetousness is questioned who its father is, it replies :—
Doubts in what the creator has predestined. An on being
asked what its occupation is, it answers :—To suffer from
the misery of exclusion."

Verses :

If thou askest covetousness, who is thy father
It says :—Doubt in the divine powers.
And if thou askest :—What is thy business ? it replies :—
To grieve over the disappointments of life.

STORY.

Sheikh Abu 'Ali Rûdbâri (m. h. s. b. s.) has said : —
"The narrowest prison is to associate with uncongenial
persons."

Verses :

Although pious men are in prison
Wherever union with the Friend is impossible,

No prison is more narrow to the anxious lover
Than the company of strangers.

STORY.

Ibráhim Khovâs (m. h. s. b. s.) has said :—" Do not grieve about what has been meted out to thee at the beginning of all things, because that is thy provision [for life], and lose not what has been required from thee, namely obedience to the commands of God; meaning things ordered to be done, or prohibited.

Verses:

Thy share has been allotted to thee from all eternity
How long wilt thou distress thyself for a livelihood ?
The object of my existence is service [of God]
Turn not away thy head from the laws of service [of God].

STORY.

Sheikh Abu-l-Hasan the butcher (m. h. s. b. s.) seeing a Darwèsh mending his robe, opening each seam which did not come right, and then sewing it again, asked :—" Perhaps this robe is thy idol ?"

Verses:

The Sûfi whose business it is to sew on patches
Does well if he indulges in the long stitches of poverty.
But impulses of nature put his hand in motion
Each thread and stitch of his becomes an idol and a string.*

---

* The word *zenâr*, string, designates the *belt* worn by eastern Christians and Jews, as well as the *Kushti* of the Zoroastrians, and the *Munj* of the Hindus. This word is used above to denote one who is no longer of the Faithful, or rather a Sûfi when he obeys the impulses of nature in his sewing i.e. in his actions.

STORY.

Hadrami (m. h. s. b. s.) said :—" A Sûfi is he who cannot be found after he has disappeared, and cannot disappear after he has been found, which [Arabic expression] means that he is a Sûfi who has become dead to the impulses of his nature and does never again obey them, because what is dead cannot be revived. Wheh however he becomes worthy of true existence and eternity after *extinction** he will not die again.

Verses :

Blessed is he, who after becoming non-existent in this meta-phoric love
No more returns to his [terrestial ?] existence
Then obtaining [another] existence, the subtle and
Eternal substance will become manifest in *extinction.†*

STORY.

Khâjah Yusuf Hamdâni (m. h. s. b. s.) was one day preaching in the Nizamiah [mosque] of Baghdâd, when a well known theologian Ibnu-l-Baqâ by name, got up and asked him some question, but he replied :—Sit down, I detect a smack of infidelity in thy words; probably thou wilt not die in the religion of Islâm." Some time afterwards this theologian became a Christian, and died as such.

Verses :

When thou seest a man, after making profession of poverty
Ranked with the pious, and his name held up as an example

---

* The word is *fanâ* which is the 8th and last stage in the Sûfi's jour-ney, corresponding to the *Nirvâna* of the Hindus, and more particularly Buddhists.

† Here the word *'adam* is used to designate non-existence, extinction, and absorption into the Deity, and not *fanâ* as above.

Raise no objections against him O friend ; lest
On account of such incivility thy religion may be wrecked.

STORY.

Khâjah 'Abu-l-Khâleq (the mercy of Allah be upon him)
was once told by a Darwêsh that if God were to give him
a choice of approbation between paradise and hell, he would
select the latter, because [a desire for] paradise implies [the
gratification of] lust, and hell implies a wish for [obedience
to] God. The Khâjah demurred to this sentiment and
exclaimed :—" What has a servant of God to do with
choosing ? Wherever He tells us to go we go, or to remain
we remain.

Verses :

Do nothing without the approbation of the Lord
O thou who professest to serve Him.
Wherever the approbation of the Lord is
What concern have His servants with approbation ?

STORY.

Khajah 'Ali being asked for the favour of saying what
Faith is, replied :—It is to uproot and to join."

Verses :

Whoever told thee that Faith is to dig up and unite
Thou must approve of his laudable definition.
What is the meaning of to uproot and to join ?
It is to sever thy heart from creatures and unite it to the
creator.

STORY.

Behâ-uddîn Naqshbandi having been asked how far his

chain [of ancestors] reached, replied that nobody can reach his destination by a chain.

Verses :

The habit and the staff [of the mendicant] will not bring on truth nor purity,

And the rosary will only suggest a suspicion of hypocrisy.

Do not repeat every moment how far thy chain [of lineage] reaches

Because no one can arrive at his destination by a chain.

SECOND GARDEN

Sprinkling of philosophical anemons and subtleties which have—
in consequence of gentle showers from the clouds of [divine]
bounty—grown in the soil of the hearts of sages, and
in the lands of their minds, as explained in
their records.

STORY.

In his world-conquering expedition Àlexander happened
by an excellent stratagem to obtain possession of a fort
which he then ordered to be razed. Being however informed
that there was a learned philosopher in the place, capable
of solving difficult problems, he summoned him to his
presence, and finding him to be of a repulsive aspect, exclaimed :—" What strange physiognomy and terrible figure
is this ? " The philosopher, surprised at these words, and
smiling, commented upon this amazement as follows :—

Verses :

Blame not my ugly countenance,
O thou who art void of virtue and justice,
The body is like the scabbard, and the soul the sword,
The scimitar does the work ; not the sheath.

He also said :—" Whoever does not act kindly toward
people his own skin becomes the prison of his body ; he is

so narrowly confined within his existence, that in comparison
to it a prison is an open place of delight."

Verses :

Be aware, that he who is ill humoured towards everybody
Will always be captive to a hundred troubles.
Tell not the constable to put him in prison,
For, the skin on the body of an ill natured man, is gaol
    enough for him.

He also said :—" An envious man is always grieving, and
. in strife with the creator, because whatever good falls to the
lot of others distresses him, and whatever he obtains does
not please him."

Verses :

The habit of an envious man—be his mouth filled with
    dust—
Is to find fault with the decisions of the wise ruler of the
    world
Whatever he sees in another man's grasp he bemoans,
    saying
Why was it given to him without cause? and not to me?

He also said :—" An intelligent and generous man gives
his property to friends, and a silly avaricious fellow leaves it
to be taken by foes."

Verses :

Whatever property a generous man accumulates
He devotes it all to the benefit of his friends
What a base and avaricious man gathers
Becomes after his death the prey of enemies.

He also said :—" To play off jests and buffoonery upon intelligent men, entails loss of one's own respectability, and brings on degradation."

Verses :

If thou emulatest a low fellow in manners

Thou wilt lose thy name of Rastam* for that of a wolf

Do not play the trade of a buffoon to great men

Because the dignity of thy own rank will be lost.

He also said :—" Why tyrannises over the weak, will be slain by the strong."†

Verses :

My heart ! Learn this good saying

Which I heard from those who know wise saws :—

Who draws the unrighteous sword

Will be slain by the sword of the unrighteous.

Alexander who repleted his ears with these jewels of wisdom, filled the mouth of the philosopher with jewels, and refrained from razing the fort.

STORY.

Sekander Afridûn who cast into the soil of mercy‡ only the seed of good advice, wrote the following maxim for his children :—" Days are like pages in the book of life, you must record upon them only the best acts and memorials."

---

* Rastram was a famous hero whose praises are sung in the Shâh-nâmah of Firdausi at great length.

† Here the play of words is on *sirdast* and *zabardast*, the powerless and the powerful, literally those *under the hand* and those *above the hand*.

‡ Here no doubt by *the soil of mercy*, youthful minds—supposed to be under special mercy and divine protection—are meant.

Verses :

The surface of the world is the book of life of all mortals,
Thus said a wise man who has considered it well :—
Blessed is he who in this book, which is first altogether blank
Writes good records, and leaves a good mark.

STORY.

A philosopher has said :—" I wrote forty books on philosophy and did not profit by them ; then I selected forty maxims from them, but with the same effect ; at last I picked out four from these, and found in them what I had sought.

First :—Do not trust wives as if they were men, because although a wife may be of a respectable tribe, she may not be of the kind that will suit a respectable man.

Verses :

The intellect of a woman is imperfect, and her knowledge too
Never place full confidence in her ;
If she be bad, confide not in her
And if she is good, trust her not.

Second :—Be not deceived by wealth, although it may be great, because it will pass away in the vicissitudes of time.

Verses :

Be not puffed up by riches like fools
Because wealth passes like a cloud
Although a passing cloud may shower jewels
A wise man puts no trust therein.

Third :—Confide not your hidden secret to any friend,

because it often happens that friendship is interrupted, and
turned into emnity :—

Verses :

O boy ! A secret necessary to be concealed from a foe
Thou wilt do well not to reveal it even to a friend
I have seen many who in course of capricious time
Became foes from friends, and amity to emnity turned.

Fourth :—Acquire only such knowledge, the want whereof
will make you die in sin,* abstain from all that is superfluous,
and pursue that which is necessary.

Verses :

Cultivate the knowledge which is indispensable to you
And seek not that which you can dispense with.
From the moment you acquire the indispensable knowledge,
You must not desire to act except in accordance therewith.

STORY.

Ibu Moqann'a states that when the library of the Indian
philosophers was carried on a hundred camels, and their king
asked for a diminution, one camel's load was brought to
to him. He however repeated his demand till it [the
library] was reduced to four maxims :—

First maxim :—Injunction to kings to be just.

Verses :

When the king of the world makes justice his rule of life,
His resting place will always be [serene, like] the moon
When a helpless man groans with wounded breast
And is even once ill treated by tyranny

---

* This implies that only religious knowledge is to be acquired.

The edifice of administration is in confusion,
It stands in need of justice, all else is nothing.
Second maxim :—Injunction to act righteously towards the
the people who will then be loyal.

Verses :

Oppression by the Shâh is the seed of the people's
disobedience
If you sow barley, how can you expect a harvest of wheat ?

Third maxim :—The body is kept in health by abstaining
to eat without appetite, and by rising from a meal before
satiety takes place.

Verses :

Take care to avoid the causes of repletion
And flee the disgrace of [employing] hypocritical quacks.
Approach not the table unless your bowels are empty
And leave it before they are satiated.

Fourth maxim :—Advice to women, to avoid looking at
strangers, and being looked upon by them.

Verses :

She is a [good] wife who shows not her face to a stranger
Although he may be the cynosure of all eyes ;
She must look at no man except her husband
Even if he be as [beautiful as] the moon in the sky.

STORY.

There are four sayings, uttered by four kings, four arrows
as it were, shot from one bow :—

The first is by Kesra* who said :—" I have never repented

---

* Kesra is Chosroes, a famous king of Persia, known better by the
name of " Nushirvân the just." He began to reign A.D. 630.

of what I have not said, but said much the repentance for which humbled me into dust and ashes.*

Verses :

No one repented for keeping a secret under seal
But many for having revealed it.
Remain silent ; because to sit quietly with a collected mind
Is better than speaking what will distract it.

Secondly :—The Qaisar of Rûm† said :—I have more power over what is unsaid than what is said ; meaning that I am able to say what I have not said, but unable to conceal what I have said.

Verses :

What thou scatterest is difficult [to conceal again],
Tell it not easily to thy companions
Because what thou keepest may be said [if need be]
But what thou hast said cannot be recalled.

Thirdly:—On the same subject the Khûqân‡ of China has said :—" It often happens that heedless talk is worse [in its consequences] than sorrow for restraining it."

Verses :

Each secret kept under seal in thy mind
Is not hastily to be written on the tablet of explanation,

---

* Literally :—From the repentance for which I slept in earth and blood.

† This was formerly the title of Byzantine emperors, but is by oriental authors sometimes applied to their successors, The Sultâns of Turkey.

‡ Emperor.

D

I fear the mulct thou wilt have to pay for divulging it
Will be more heavy than thy sorrow* for concealing it.
Fourthly :—The king of India has enounced this maxim :—
" The words which have escaped from my mouth are beyond
my control ; but what I have not spoken is in my possession,
and I may utter it or not, as I like.

Verses :
A sage has on a retained and divulged secret,
Uttered the following excellent simile :—
The one is like an arrow yet in the hand
The other like an arrow which has left the bow.

STORY.

A king of India sent presents to a Khalifah of Baghdâd,
and with them a physician, skilled both in medicine and
philosophy, who spoke to him as follows :—" I have brought
three things, fit only for kings and Sultâns." On being
asked to explain, he continued :—"The first is a dye by
means of which grey hair may be changed to black, so that
it will never become white. The second is a confection,
which enables a person to indulge in eating to any extent
without injuring his health. The third is an aphrodisiac,
the repeated use whereof will bring on neither weakness of
sight, nor loss of strength." The Khalifah remained silent
a while and then said :—"I imagined thee to be more
learned and intelligent than thou art, because the hair-dye

---

* In the prose the word *pashimâni* and in the verses which follow it
the word *nedâmet* is used, both of which strictly mean *repentance*, but I
rendered them by *sorrow*.

thou mentionest, ministers only to vanity and falsehood. Black hair is the symbol of darkness and white of light; who would be foolish enough to clothe light with darkness."

Verses:

The fool who dyes his grey hair black
Yet hopes to be young when he is old.
How can shrewd men who know the world*
Consider a black crow to be elegant like a white falcon !

" As to the confection of which thou hast spoken [I inform thee that] I am not of the class of men who delight in being voracious. Can there be anything more unpleasant than to be compelled every moment to go to a place to see there things not to be looked upon, to hear sounds not to be listened to, and to smell what ought not to be smelled. Wise men have said that hunger is a disease of the constitution, which is cured by meat and drink. He is a fool who makes himself purposely sick, in order to subject himself to the misery of being treated."

Verses:

The gentleman tries to acquire appetite
In order to supply a want in his constitution
And that he may with cooked and raw things
As much as required, satisfy that want.

" As to the aphrodisiac thou hast mentioned [I tell thee that] dalliance with women is a kind of mental derangement

---

* The literal translation of the phrase is :—" Learned men who are the bonds of fortune-hunting," which is rather awkward.

far from the dictates of reason. And how would the Khalifah of the world look on his knees before a girl, flattering
her and displaying hypocrisy ? "

Verses :

O thou who boastest of intellect how long wilt thou in lust
Grasp the curls of thy mistress and court insanity ?
What more foolish canst thou do, than to be on thy knees
Before a Zangi* shaking thy posterior ?

STORY.

In the assembly of Kesra, three philosophers, one a
Rûmi, the other a Hindu and the third Barzachumihr† discussed various topics, and when the question, of what was
the most unfortunate thing, came up, the Rûmi said :—" Old
age, weakness, poverty and distress." The Hindu said :—
" A sick body with abundance of grief." Barzachumihr
said :—" Proximity of death with an absence of good actions." All agreed thereon that Barzachumihr was right.

Verses :

Intelligent philosophers queried near Kesra
About the heaviest wave in this abyss of grief,‡
The first said it must be sickness and long pain ;
The second averred, it is the union of old age and poverty,
The third said, it is the nearness of death without good
    deeds,
And to him the palm of victory was awarded.

---

* A native of Zanzibar in particular, and an African negro in general.
† Literally, *Bright as the sun.* He was the celebrated wazir of Kesra
Nushirvân.
‡ Simile of this world.

STORY.

A philosopher having been asked, when human beings ought to make haste to eat, replied :—"A rich man whenever he feels hungry, and a poor one whenever he finds something to eat."

Verses :

Eat in such a way that thy body
Be not ruined by excess or deficiency
If thou hast food, eat when thou listest
If not, be patient, eat when thou hast it.

STORY.

A philosopher enjoined his son not to leave the house in the morning without having partaken of some food, because it begets patience and forbearance, whereas hunger gives rise to ill-humour and a hasty temper.

Verses :

Do not make thy humour impatient by fasting,
Because meekness and forbearance surpass all things,
If fasting becomes an occasion of trouble
Then the breaking of it is better than the keeping.

Maxim.

When thou art hungry thou wilt find any kind of food or bread appetising to thy nature, and the friends with whom thou art sitting will be charmed by thy society.*

Verses :

Whatever moist or dry thou findest in the house
It is better that thou eat of it to satiety

---

* Or :—The friends with whom thou art sitting will share in thy appetite.

Than that thou shouldst covet the food of others
Or greedily hope for doles from good men.

Maxim.

When the host takes a seat at the edge of the table, and sees [as it were] himself [laid out] on it [apprehending that thou wilt eat him up], then it would be better for thee to eat of thy own liver than of his food, and to drink of thy own blood, than to partake of his table's hospitality.

Verses :

When a man says :—" *My* table, and *my* bread " withdraw
Thy foot from his table, and thy hand from his bread ;
The greens thou eatest from thy own garden
Are sweeter than his roasted lamb.

Maxim.

Who has been granted the enjoyment of the following five things, has the reins of a happy life in his hand :—1st, Health of body. 2nd, Liberty. 3rd, Abundant income. 4th, A kind friend. 5th, Leisure ; and whoever is deprived of these has the door of a pleasant existence locked against him.

Verses :

The causes of a happy life amount to five
According to the opinions of celebrated sages :—
Leisure, liberty, health, a sufficient income
A virtuous and good-natured companion.

Maxim.

Any blessing that decreases or perishes is not accounted as one by a wise man ; and as life, although it may be long, also ends with death, the duration of it is of no use.   Noah (to whom be salutation) lived a thousand years in the world, and up to this day five thousand have elapsed since he died. That blessing has value which is eternal and suffers no diminution.

Verses :

A wise man considers that a blessing
Which rejoices the heart for ever and ever.
The tomb will be thy resting place ; hence silver and gold
Will remain on the top of it like stones.

Maxim.

Barzachumihr having been asked who the most virtuous king is, replied :—" He from whom the virtuous are secure, but whom the wicked fear."

Verses :

He is a [virtuous] Shâh who is enlightened and wise,
Causing the state of the good to be good, and of the bad to
    be bad.

STORY.

Hejâj* having been advised to fear God and not to oppress Musalmâns, was also a very eloquent orator, and having ascended the pulpit said :—" God the Most High has appointed me over you with [the duty of producing] awe ! Considering your acts you will not be delivered from oppression when I die. God the Most High possesses many servants like myself, and in case I should die, it is possible that one worse than myself will arrive."

---

* Name of a governor notorious for his tyranny.

Verses :

If thou wantest the Shâh to be just, be just thyself
In thy dealings, which are the field of thy activity.*
The Shâh is a mirror, whatever thou seest therein
Is only the reflection of thy own mode of acting.

Maxim.

A Pâdshâh asked a philosopher for advice, but the latter requested permission to put a question ; and this having been granted he queried :—" Dost thou love gold more, or a foe ?" He replied :—" Gold." The philosopher continued :—" The thing thou lovest, namely gold, thou wilt leave here [when thou diest] and him whom thou doest not love, namely the foe [or rather the guilt incurred by extorting gold] thou wilt carry with thee [to the next world]." Thereon the Pâdshâh wept and said :—" Thou hast given me good advice, and [the essence of] every advice."—

Verses :

Thou excitest a thousand kinds of enmity among the people
    of the world
By thy extreme greediness for silver and gold.
Gold and silver are thy friends, but their possessor is the
    enemy
From whose hand thou wrestest them by force and fraud ;
Prudence does not enjoin, nor intellect demand
That thou abandon thy friend, and take with thee thy foe.

STORY.

Alexander degraded one of his officials by removing him

---

* Literally :— " The battlefield of thy take and give."

from a high and employing him in a low post. One day
this man waited upon Alexander, who asked him what he
thought of his occupation, and he replied :—" May the life
of my Lord be long, a man is not ennobled by a great occupation, but an occupation is ennobled by a great man. In
every post honesty, justice and equity are needed." Alexander was pleased with this opinion, and re-installed him in
his former office.

Verses :

If thou desirest a high post, be careful
To practice virtue and honesty ;
The greatness of a man is not in his post,
But the post is made great by the man.

Maxim.

Three things are unbecoming in three kinds of men :—
Haste in a king, greediness in a scholar, and avarice in a
plutocrat :—

Verses :

These three things are written down bad
By the pen of the recorder in three men :—
A hasty temper in a powerful king,
Covetousness in a scholar, avarice in a rich man.

Maxim.

Wise men have said that by justice the world is rendered
populous, and by oppression deserted. Justice sheds light
to a thousand Farsangs* in its own direction, and oppres-

---

* The Farsang differs in various localities, but is generally reckoned
to amount to about 4½ or 5 English miles.

sion emits darkness from its centre to a thousand Farsangs.

Verses :

Cultivate justice ; for, when its morn dawns
The splendour thereof extends to 1000 Farsangs ;   •
But when the darkness of tyranny manifests itself
The world is filled with gloom, destitution and misery.

STORY.

A strong-minded Darwêsh, who was in the habit of fre-
quently paying visits to a king of great dignity, observed
one day signs of weariness on his countenance, and after
endeavouring to discover the cause, arrived at the conclusion
that it must be the frequency of his own attendance ; accordingly he ceased his visits. In course of time the king
happened to meet him, and asked him why he had interrupted
his attendance. The Darwêsh replied :—" Because I know
that it is preferable to be asked for the reason of not coming,
than to perceive signs of weariness for coming."

Verses :

That rich man said to the Darwêsh :—" Why
Hast thou not come so long a time ? "
He said :—" Because I would rather be asked
Why I had not come, than why I had come."

THIRD GARDEN

*Explanation of the blooming of blossoms from the plantation
of government and administration, which contains fruits
of justice and equity, to show that the wisdom of
Sultâns consists in the practice of righteousness,
and not in the display of pomp and glory.*

Although Nushirvân was a stranger to religion he was
unique in justice and uprightness, so that the prince of
created beings (upon whom be the most excellent benedictions) has said, boasting :—" I was born in the time of the
just king Nushirvân."*

Verses :
The prophet who in the reign of Nushirvân
Became the eye and the lamp of the world,
Has said :—" I am preserved from tyranny,
For I was born in the time of Nushirvân."
How well did that kind adviser say
Into the heart of a tyrannic king :—

---

* Kesra Nushirvân, the just, was a Zoroastrian, and Muhammad was
born during his reign.

" Be on thy guard of the darkness of tyranny,
Practice justice for an experiment,
If justice does not pay better than tyranny
Thou mayst again oppression try."

STORY.

It is recorded in chronicles that Guebres and Moghs*
enjoyed dominion for five thousand years, which remained
in their dynasty because they governed their subjects justly,
and tolerated no oppression.

Maxim.

There is a tradition that God the Most High sent the
following revelation to David (salutation to him) :—" Tell
thy people not to speak evil of the kings of Persia, nor to
insult them, because they made the world populous through
justice, that my worshippers may live at ease therein."

Verses :

Be aware that justice and equity, not unbelief nor religion
Are needed for the maintenance of the kingdom.
Justice without religion is for the next world
Better than the tyranny of a religious Shâh.

Maxim.

A king needs for a companion a sage who practises
wisdom, and not a courtier addicted to frivolity, because
the former will try to perfect, and the latter to damage everything within his influence.

---

* Zoroastrians and Magi.

Verses :

Every [wise] maxim uttered by the mouth and teeth is a jewel

Happy is he, who has made of his breast a casket of jewels;

A sage is a treasury of the jewels of philosophy,

Do not separate thyself from this treasure.

STORY.

One morning a Mobed of Mobeds* accompanied Qobâd† whose charger happened during the ride to defile his hind-quarters most disgracefully, whereat Qobâd became dis-pleased, and asked his companion to tell him something on the rules of behaviour in the cavalcade of a Sultân, whereon the Mobed said :—" One of them is that during the night, the morning after which the king is to ride out, his charger is not to be fed to such a degree as to cause him incon-venience." Qobâd approved of what he had said, but also told him that this ingenious suggestion of his, had been prompted by what had just happened.

Verses :

The wise man who follows the dictates of nature

Will in all matters behave according to truth and propriety;

But the intelligent man who acts according to reason

Will by his ingenuity teach good manners even to animals.

---

* Zoroastrian Highpriest, and also court dignitary.

† Ascended the throne for the first time A.D. 487, and again, the 2nd time after Jamasp, A.D. 9.

Maxim.

The favourites of Sultâns are like people climbing up a precipitous mountain, and falling off from it in consequence of the quakes of anger and the vicissitudes of time. There is no doubt that the fall of those who are higher up, is more disastrous, than the coming down of those who are in lower positions.

Verses :

The seat of proximity to the Sultân is high,
Those placed on it are very exalted ;
I fear when thou fallest from that height
Thou wilt fall more heavily than all others.

Maxim.

Sovereigns ought secretly to employ men who act and speak justly, in order to bring under their notice the circumstances of their distressed subjects and agriculturists. Aradashir* is said to have been so well-informed a king, that when his courtiers arrived in the morning, he told them what a certain man had been eating, or how a certain woman had behaved towards a girl, and the like ; so that the people imagined that some angel from heaven must be paying him visits, and informing him what they were doing. Mahmûd Sabaktagîn was also of that kind.

Verses :

If the Shâh be not aware of his army's state
How can the soldiers avoid the severity of winter !

---

* There were three Ardashirs in the Sasanian dynasty, but it is not said which of them is meant here.

They have a thousand excuses for quaffing wine,
They sing a thousand songs; profligacy tuning the lute.

STORY.

Aristotle has said, that the best king is he, who is like a vulture surrounded by carrion, and not like carrion surrounded by vultures ; that is to say, he must be aware of the affairs of those around him, and they must be ignorant of his; but not the contrary.

Verses :

A king must be informed like a vulture
Because corpses have fallen round him,
Not like a corpse around which vultures assemble
With sharpened beaks, to derive profit from him.

STORY.

On new year's day, Nushirvân holding a reception with a lovely damsel* by his side, perceived an individual connected with him, purloining a golden bowl and concealing it in his armpit, but pretended not to see it and said nothing. When the assembly broke up, the cupbearer desired that no one should leave the place because he had missed a bowl and intended to search for it. Nushirvân however beckoned to him, to let the matter drop ; saying that he who had taken the cup would not restore it, and who had seen the theft would not reveal it. Some days afterwards the same individual again made his appearance at court, dressed in

---

* The expression is *bâ mihr jân-efrûz*, literally :—*With a soul illuminating sun.*

new garments, and with new shoes on his feet. Nushirvân
pointing to his robe, asked :—" Is this from that ? " and the
culprit lifting up the skirts from the shoes replied :—" These
also are from that." Nushirvân smiled, and knowing that
distress had impelled him to commit the act, ordered a
thousand Misqâls* to be presented to him.

Verses :

When a noble Shâh becomes aware of thy transgression
Confess thy fault and hope for pardon from his magnanimity.
Deny not thy sin ; by doing so thou committest another .
Which is far worse than the first.

STORY.

Mâmûn† had a slave, who, having been put in charge of
the water for purification, lost after a few days the ewer and
the washing-basin. One day Mâmûn said :—" I wish thou
wouldst sell to me also the ewer and the basin thou carriest."
He replied :—" I shall do so."—" What wilt thou take for
the basin which is here ? "—" Ten dinârs."‡ Accordingly
he ordered ten dinârs to be given to the slave, and said :—
" Now this basin has been made safe ;" and the slave assented.

Verses :

Do not grudge silver to one whom thou hast purchased with
    gold§

---

* A Misqâl of gold is 68⁴ grains in weight.

† Mâmûn, the Khalifah of Baghdâd, reigned from the 28th March
812, till the 30th July, 833.

‡ Name of a gold coin.

§ A slave is meant whose value is considerable.

That his soul may be thereby set at rest;
Acquiesce in ransoming thy body with money,
That thou mayest not lose thy life at last.

STORY.

Great friendship subsisted between Mo'aviah* and 'Oqail, the son of Abu Tâleb; but in course of time a thorn fell upon the path of their love, dust settled upon the countenance of their affection, so that 'Oqail ceased to pay visits to Mo'aviah, and withdrew his feet from the assembly of the latter. Thereon Mo'aviah wrote to him :—" O aim [*matlab*] of the tribe of 'Abdu-l-mutallab, O final [*aqsa*] intention of the family of Qossa, O opener of the musk-bag [*nâfah*] of 'Abd Manâf,† O source of noble deeds of the Beni Hâshem, the miracle of prophetship belongs to' thee, and the honour of apostleship is in thy family.· Where has all that magnanimity, gentleness and forbearance departed to? Return, for I am penitent for what has taken place, and distressed for what has been said [by me]."

Verses :

How long shall I be the target of the arrow of remorse
And remain deprived of heart and religion whilst thou art
 far ;
Whilst I am on earth, my face is before thee also on the
 earth,
Under the earth I shall likewise be thus [humbly prostrated].

---

* Mo'aviah I., the first Ommiade Khalifah, reigned from A.D. 661 till 679.

† The play on the words *matlab Mutallab*, *aqsa Qossa*, and *nâfah Manâf* could be indicated above but slightly.

The reply which 'Oqail wrote to him.

Verses :

Thou hast spoken the truth ; thy heart is true, but I
Am of opinion that I should not see thee, nor thou me ;
I do not say anything against a friend,
But I turn away from him who insults me.

He means [by these verses, which are in Arabic] that when
a noble fellow becomes displeased with a friend, he is to
betake himself to 'the corner of separation and to walk
about in the street of exile, but not to gird his loins to evil,
and to utter calumnies.

Verses :

When a friend desires to quarrel with thee
Do nothing ; but court separation from him,
Do not strive much to produce enmity
But abandon friendship by degrees.

Mo'aviah again endeavoured to reconcile him with excuses
in order to induce him to make peace, and sent him for
that purpose a thousand dirhems.*

Verses :

Excuse thyself and beg pardon from thy friends
When a breach arises in the foundation of amity among
      friends,
And if the breach cannot be repaired by word of speech
Endeavour to build it up by employing bricks of silver and
      gold.

---

* Dirhem is derived from the Greek Drahma, and was a silver coin.

STORY.

In a hunting party Hejâj was separated from his retinue, and ascending a hill observed an Arab of the desert, who sat there and was engaged in picking out insects from his ragged garments, whilst his camels were browsing around him. When the camels caught sight of Hejâj, they scampered off, whereon the man looked up and angrily exclaimed :—"Who is this coming up in this desert with a shining robe. A curse be upon him !" Hejâj remained silent, but afterwards approached and said :—" Peace be upon thee O Arab of the desert !" He replied :—" No peace to thee, neither the mercy of Allah, nor His benedictions." Then Hejâj asked him for water, and he replied :—" Alight humbly, and drink water submissively ; for by Allah, I am the companion and servant of nobody." Hejâj alighted, drank water, and then asked :—" O Arab of the desert ! Who is the best of men ? " He replied :—" The apostle of God, the benediction of Allah be upon him, upon his family and peace." He again asked :—" What sayest thou concerning 'Ali* the son of Abu Tâleb ?" He replied :—"His generosity and magnanimity are such that language is too imperfect to express them."† " What sayest thou about 'Abdu-l-Melik the son of Mervân ?"‡ He remained silent, whereon Hejâj reiterated :—" Give me a reply, O Arab of

---

* Cousin, son-in-law, and first convert of the prophet.

† Literally :—They are such that the mouth cannot hold them.

‡ This Ommiade Khalifah reigned from A.D. 684 till 705.

E 2

the desert."—" He is a bad man."—He queried :—" Why ?"
the Arab replied :—" He has committed a fault, in consequence of which he is detested from the east to the west."
—" What is it ? "—He said :—" Because he has appointed
that wicked and profligate Hejâj to govern Musalmâns."
Hejâj said nothing ; meanwhile a little bird suddenly flut-
tered up, giving forth a sound, whereon the Arab turned
towards Hejâj and said :—" Who art thou, O man " Hejâj
replied :—" What a question is this thou askest ? " The
Arab continued :—" This bird informs me that an army is
about to arrive, of which thou art the commander." Whilst
they were thus conversing the troops arrived and saluted
Hejâj. When the Arab perceived this, the hue of his face
changed, and Hejâj ordered the man to be taken into his
retinue. The next morning when breakfast was laid out
and the people assembled, Hejâj called for the Arab, who
on entering said ;—" Peace be upon thee, O Amir, with the
mercy of Allah, and his benedictions." Hejâj replied :—
" I do not say as thou hast said, peace be upon thee," and
then asked him whether he should like to eat ? " The Arab
replied :—" The food is thine, and if allowed I shall do so."
Permission having been given, the Arab exclaimed :—" Bis-
millah and Inshallah,* and may that which comes after the
food be good." Hejâj smiled, and [turning to his guests]
asked :—" Do you know what happened yesterday between

---

* *In the name of Allah* and *if it pleaseth Allah* expressions used by
good Moslems at the commencement of anything.

me and this fellow ?" The Arab said :—" May Allah prosper thee, O Amir, of not divulge to-day the secret which took place yesterday between us, because [the proverb says] what is past is not mentioned." Then Hejâj continued :— " O Arab of the desert, choose one of these two things ; either remain with me that I may make thee one of my courtiers, or I shall send thee to ' Abdu-l-Melik, the son of Mervân, and inform him of what thou hast said about him." The Arab said :—" There may be yet another way." Hejâj asked :—" What is it ?" He continued :—" To let me depart in peace to my country, so that thou mayest see me no more, nor I thee." Hejâj then laughed, ordered him to be presented with ten thousand dinârs and to be sent to his country.

Verses :

A man must with polite language and graceful address
Restrain a tyrant from practicing oppression ;
Every base clown far from generosity and liberality
Brings him back to liberality by deceitful words.

STORY.

Yezdegird* had noticed his son Behrâm in a place of the Harem which was not proper ; whereon he told him to go out, to administer thirty lashes to the chamberlain, to remove him from his post at the door-curtain of the inner apartments, and to substitute another chamberlain, whose name he mentioned, in his place. Behrâm executed the bidding

---

* Here Yezdegird II. is meant, who ascended the throne A.D. 399.

of his father ; but being at that time not older than thirteen years of age, knew not the reason of his father's displeasure with the chamberlain. Next day he went again to the door of the inner apartments and desired to enter, but the chamberlain placed a hand against his breast and demurred, telling him that if he again trespassed at this spot, he would give him thirty lashes for the treachery he had committed against the former chamberlain. When this encounter was brought to the notice of Yezdegird, he approved of the chamberlain's behaviour, and presented him with a robe of honour.

Verses :

The Shâh is to be so guarded, that to overstep his threshold
Must not enter the head of a slave nor a freeman.
To the sanctuary of his honour which is the seat of dominion
No bird can fly, no wind can penetrate.

STORY.

The Vezier of Hormuz, son of Shâpûr* wrote him a letter, saying that merchants of the sea had brought many jewels, which he purchased for 100,000 dinârs on behalf of the king; but if it be true, as he had heard, that his majesty was unwilling to take them, a certain trader would be ready to re-purchase them [at a much higher price] and leave a clear gain of 100,000 dinârs to the king. Hormuz wrote in reply : " With us 100,000 dinârs are not of much account, and if we engage in commerce the question is, who will govern, and what will the merchants do? "

---

* This is Hormur I., whose reign began A.D. 271.

Verses :

It is not in conformity with the dignity of kings
To engage in trade in order to gain a livelihood.
If the Shâh makes the business of merchants his own
Say thyself, what else will traders do after that !

STORY.

'Omar,* the commander of the Faithful (the approbation
of Allah be upon him) being during his Khalifate in Medinah engaged in plastering a wall with mud, was waited
upon by a Jew who complained that the governor of Bosrah
had purchased from him goods to the amount of 100,000
dirhems but was tardy in repaying the value. 'Omar called
for paper but† none being procurable, he took up a potsherd
and wrote on it :—"Those who complain against thee are
numberless, and those who thank thee cannot be found.
Either cease to give cause for complaint, or vacate thy post
of governor." The signature of " 'Omer Ibnu-l-Khettâb "
was appended, but neither a seal nor a Joghra,‡ nevertheless
the power and justice of the government of 'Omar were so
great, and the awe he inspired so general, that on the mere
presentation of the said potsherd, the governor of Bosrah
alighted from his horse, prostrated himself to the ground,
and fully satisfied all the demands of the Jew, who remained
sitting on his animal.

---

* 'Omar was Khalifah from A.D. 634 till 643.

† No doubt Egyptian *papyrus*, real paper not having yet been invented at that early time.

‡ This calligraphic writing used in titles, &c., was not yet invented
in 'Omar's time.

Verses:

When the Shâh enjoys the authority of government
He shields an abject fellow from the hands of the insolent;
But when a lion sheds his teeth and claws,
Lame foxes box his ears !

STORY.

A youth having been caught in a theft, the Khalifah said:
" Cut off his hand, that it may be shortened from [stealing]
the goods of Musalmâns." The culprit wept and said :—

Verses:

As God has adorned me with the right hand and the left
Permit not thy eye to swerve from what is right.

The Khalifah repeated the injunction, saying that it is one
of the ordinances of God the Most High, in which Musalmâns have no option. The mother of the youth, who was
present, rose and said :—" O Khalifah ! This is my son
by whose aid I live from morning till night, and by whose
labour I am supported."

Verses:

The son is, as it were, giving life
To my much oppressed soul.
His hand is the mainstay of my support,
Do not approve of its amputation.

The Khalifah said :—" Cut off his hand, because I do not
pardon his crime, and do not mean to incur the guilt of
having neglected this ordinance." The mother of the youth
said :—" Consider this [guilt] like any of thy other sins, for
which thou art always craving pardon and praying to be for-

given." The Khalifah being pleased with this remark said : " Let him alone."

Verses :

Happy is that learned man who in the presence of the Shâh
Utters a pleasant maxim when he is inflamed with anger,
When like water he brings the graceful maxim
To the Shâh, it throws water upon fire.

STORY.

A culprit having been brought before the Khalifah, he ordered the punishment due to the transgression to be administered. The prisoner said :—" O commander of the Faithful, to take vengeance for a crime is justice, but to pass it over is virtue ; and the magnanimity of the prince of the Faithful is more exalted, than that he should disregard what is higher, and descend to what is lower." The Khalifah being pleased with this argument, condoned his transgression.

Verses :

To pardon a crime is virtue, to punish it is justice.
The former is distant from the latter, like heaven from earth.
How could one abandon virtue and follow justice,
Who is wise enough to know the difference between them.

STORY.

A stripling of the Beni Hâshem* having been disrespectful to a man of rank, was taken to his uncle who intended to punish him. The boy said :—" O my uncle ! I acted as

---

* Name of a celebrated tribe of Arabs.

I did because wisdom was not with me. Do thou what thou listest, because wisdom is with thee."

Verses :

If a fool obeys the behests of passion and humour
And does not act according to the dictates of reason,
As humour and passion have not conquered thee
Never walk on any other path except that of reason.

STORY.

A woman who belonged to the faction which had risen in arms against Hejâj, having been brought before him, he spoke to her, but she looked down, and fixing her eyes upon the ground, neither replied, nor glanced at him. One who was present said :—"O woman ! The Amir is speaking, and thou lookest away?" She replied :—" I am ashamed before God the Most High, to look on a man, upon whom God the Most High does not look."

Verses :

Look not at the countenance of a tyrant
Because it is an open door to hell.
Till the eye of God has not been opened towards him
No act of mercy has fallen from him.

STORY.

Alexander having been asked by what means he had attained such dominion, power and glory at so youthful an age and during so short a reign, replied :—" By reconciliating foes till they turned away from the path of enmity, and by strengthening the alliances with friends till they became firm in the bonds of amity."

Verses :

If thou wantest the kingdom of Alexander, thou must by
good behaviour -
Make friends of thy foes, and friends more friendly stilL

STORY.

One day whilst Alexander was sitting with his officers, one
of them said :—"God the Most' High has bestowed upon
thee a great monarchy ; take many wives unto thee, that thy
progeny may become numerous to perpetuate thy memory
in the world." He replied:—"My memory and my children
will be my good words and my excellent examples. It is
not fit that he who conquered men in the world, should
be vanquished by women."

Verses :

A father cannot be certain whether his son
Will be of the crowd of fools or intelligent;
The good conduct of a sage is a sufficient progeny to him,
Why should he for the hope of children be subject to a wife?

FOURTH GARDEN

Fruitfulness of the trees of liberality and generosity with their shedding of blossoms in the shape of gifts in dirhems and dinârs.

The beauty* of liberality consists in bestowing gifts without interest and without expecting an equivalent for them, although that interest or equivalent may be either praise [in this world] or an abundant reward [in the next world].

Verses :

Who is liberal?   He whose every good act
Is done by him for [gaining approbation from] God ;
What is done for [gaining worldly] praise and reward
Take it to be a purchase and sale of the blessings of existence.

Verses :

Whose liberality is prompted by the intention
To obtain a great name in the world,
His house is outside the gates
Of the region of liberality and city of benevolence.

---

* The word used in the text is literally *profit*, and I figuratively translate it by *beauty*.

STORY.

A liberal man, having been asked whether he felt any inward gratification, or received any thanks from needy persons and mendicants upon whom he bestowed largesses, replied sighing :—" In my bounties and liberalities my duty is only that of a ladle in the hands of a cook ; whatever he distributes is done by the instrumentality of the ladle, but how can the ladle presume to be the giver 1 "

Verses :

Although the daily food comes from the gentleman, the
. giver of it is God,
It is not fair that he should expect thanks from those who
consume it,
He is but the cup and spoon of the cauldron of food
It is better for the bowl and ladle to receive no thanks.

STORY.

One Sûfi described another, and, adducing some of his qualifications in the way of knowledge [see footnote on page 10], said, that when giving a banquet, although the possessor, he does not consider himself as the sharer or host of it, treats all his guests in the same way, and considers himself as one of the *uninvited.**

Verses :

When in his guesthouse a gentleman
Sets out a table for poor persons

---

* The word is *Jufeel*, and such a guest being generally also· bashful and retiring was therefore by the Romans called a shadow, *umbra.*

He is but a *child* on the path [of Sûfi doctrines]
Unless he considers himself as one of the *uninvited guests.**

STORY.

An Arab of the desert once made his appearance in the
house of 'Ali the Amir of the Faithful — who was the
prince of liberal men of ancient and of modern times, may
Allah be pleased with him and ennoble his countenance—
and sat down quietly, but the shyness of misery and poverty
had put their stamp on his brow, so that when His Excellency the Amir of the Believers asked him what he wanted,
he was ashamed to speak, but wrote on the ground that he
was destitute. Accordingly, as he had nothing else, he presented him with two pieces of cloth, one of which the Arab
immediately put on as a mantle, and the other as a loin-cloth.
Then standing up he recited some beautiful and perfectly eloquent distichs appropriate to the occasion, which so pleased
His Excellency the Amir that he added to his gift thirty dinârs
which belonged to his sons the Amirs of the Faithful, Hasan
and Husain—may Allah be pleased with them—and which
he had been keeping for them. The Arab took the money,
averred that 'Ali had made him the wealthiest man of his
house, and took leave. His Excellency the Amir said :—
"I have heard the lord of apostleship† say that *the price of
everything is according to its beauty*, which means that the

---

* The play on the words *Jifl*, child, and *Jufeel*, cannot be expressed
in English.
† The prophet Muhammad.

value of every man is according to what adorns him of good acts, and of pithy maxims.

Verses :

The price of a man consists not in silver and gold
.The value of a man is his power and virtue ;
Many a slave has by acquiring virtue
Attained much greater power than a gentleman,
And many a gentleman has for want of virtue
Become *inferior* to his own slave.*

STORY.

It is on record that 'Abdullah Ibn J'afer (may Allah be pleased with him) intended one day to travel, and approaching a date-grove where he had seen some persons, he alighted. The guardian of the trees happened to be a black slave, to whom two loaves of bread had just been sent from the house ; and as a dog stood near him, he threw one of the loaves to it, which having been devoured by the animal, he gave away also the other, and the dog likewise consumed it, then 'Abdullah (m. A. b. p. w. h.) asked what his daily allowance was? The slave replied :—" Whát thou hast seen."—" Then why hast thou not kept it for thyself ?"—" The dog is a stranger here ; I thought he was coming from a long distance and hungry, wherefore I did not mean to leave him in that condition."—" Then what wilt thou eat to day?"—" I shall fast." Then 'Abdullah said to him-

---

* I translate *inferior*, but the Persian has for the sake of the metre, *without a shield*, which of course implies weakness and inferiority.

self :—" Everybody is blaming me for my liberality, and
this slave is more liberal than myself." Then he purchased
both the slave and the date-grove, presenting him with the
latter, and emancipating him :—

Verses :

Who presents a dog with a piece or two of bread
To appease the cravings of his hunger,
Although he may be only a slave,
Gentlemen must bow to him as slaves.

STORY.

There was in Madinah a scholar and official, perfect in
all the sciences, who happened one day to pass through the
quarter of the workers in brass, where he caught sight of a
singing girl, the beauty of whose countenance excited the
envy of the planet Venus and of the sun. He fell madly
in love with her attractions, distracted by her curls and her
mole. Listening to her songs he was transported from the
regions of existence into the desert of annihilation, and the
hearing of her melodies carried him from the confinement
of intelligence int) the vast avenues of dementia :—

Verses :

Beauty of face and voice
Each alone ravishes the heart,
Both however combined in one
Perplex the affairs of pious men.

He threw away the garment of scholarship, and donned
the sackcloth of disgrace, relaxed his manners, and roamed
about the lanes and bâzârs of Madinah. Friends reproved

him, but in vain, and he vented his feelings in the following words :—

Verses :
When the heart-ravisher thus displays her charms
How can a lover elude the calamity.
The reproach of people is a wind to my ear
But a wind which only fans my flame.

This affair having been narrated to 'Abdullah Ibn J'afer, he called the owner of the girl, purchased her for 40,000 dinârs, and ordered her to sing in the same manner as she had captivated the above mentioned scholar. On asking her from whom she had learnt the melody, she mentioned another girl, who was thereon summoned to his presence, and the scholar likewise. Then the second girl was ordered to sing the melody, whereon the scholar immediately fainted, so that all believed he had expired. Now 'Abdullah Ibn J'afer said :—" Behold the crime we committed by killing this man." Then he ordered water, and essence of roses to be sprinkled upon the face of the man—who then recovered —and said :—"We knew not that love for that girl had overpowered thee so much." He replied :—" By Allah ! What is concealed is more than that which has become manifest." 'Abdullah then asked him whether he wished to hear the melody from the girl herself, and the man replied :—" Thou hast seen what befel me from hearing the melody sung by a girl whom I do not love. What will be my condition if I hear it from the lips of my own mistress ?"

F

—'Abdullah asked :—" If thou seest her wilt thou know her ? " He wept and said :

Verses :

Thou askest whether I shall know her who robbed me of my heart and Faith ?

By Allah ! I know no one in the world besides her.

'Abdullah ordered the girl to be brought out, and presenting her to the man he said :—" She belongs to thee, for I have not looked upon her except from the corner of my eye." The scholar prostrated himself at the feet of 'Abdullah and said :—

Verses :

Thou hast magnanimously relieved my distress
And brought me to the shore from the waves of separation,
Thou hast brought peace to my heart from the pangs of grief,
Thou hast given sleep to my weeping eyes.

Then he took possession of the girl and departed to his house, and 'Abdullah sent a slave with 40,000 dinârs after them, so as to relieve them from the cares of maintenance, and enable them to enjoy each other with untrammelled minds.

STORY.

During the reign of Mo'aviah one thousand dirhems were annually given to 'Abdullah Ibn J'afer from the public treasury, but when Yazid succeeded to the Khalifate, this sum was augmented to five thousand, whereon he was blamed for giving to one man what belonged to the com-

munity of Musalmâns ; but Yazid replied that in reality he
was giving it to all the poor of Madinah, because 'Abdullah
turns none of them away. In fact, when a man was secretly
despatched to follow him to Madinah, it appeared that he
had within the space of one month disbursed the whole sum,
and was borrowing money :—

Verses :

If the whole world falls into the possession of a liberal man
What is the world, and a hundred bâzârs of the world
    besides ?   .
Why should the heart of a Darwêsh be dismayed?
Since the purse of his liberality is the treasury of the Dar-
    wêsh.

STORY.

A Khalifah of Baghdâd was progressing with his retinue
in great splendour, when a lunatic encountered him and
said :—" O Khalifah, keep in thy reins ; I have composed
three distichs in thy praise." On being asked to recite
them he did so, and the Khalifah was pleased. When the
lunatic saw this he said :—" Favour me with three dirhems
that I may buy oil and dates, to eat my fill." The Khalifah
ordered a thousand dirhems to be given him for each
distich.

Verses :

When the misery of want oppresses an eloquent man
It is meet for him to eulogise a liberal king,
He who is praised being generous ; if for the poem's
Every distich he gives a jewel from his treasury, it is proper.

F 2

STORY.

Ibrahim Ibn Sulaimân Ibn 'Abdu-l-Melik says :—"At
the time when the Khalifate devolved from the Bani Omay-
yah upon the Bani 'Abbâs, the latter captured the former
and slew them. I happened once to be seated outside
of Kufah, on the flat roof of a building, with a prospect
upon the desert, and seeing black flags issue from Kufah,
imagined that the crowd had come in search of me. I
descended from the roof, but knew at the time no one in
Kufah in whose house I might conceal myself; and reach-
ing a large edifice I beheld a handsome individual stationed
there on horseback, surrounded by slaves and attendants.
I saluted him, and when he asked me who I was and what
I wanted, I told him that I was a fugitive dreading an
enemy and had taken refuge near his house. He then took
me inside, and allotted me a room which was near his Harem.
There I spent some days most comfortably, being provided
with the food and drink I liked best, as well as with clothes.
My host asked me no questions, but rode out once daily and
returned again. When I inquired for what reason he thus
went out, he said :—' Ibrâhim Ibn Sulaimân has killed my
father, and I heard that he is in concealment; accordingly I
sally forth every day with the hope to find him, and to avenge
upon him the murder of my father.'—When I heard these
words I was amazed at my misfortune and at the decree of
fate, which had thrown me into the house of the very man
who desired to kill me. This made me weary of life, and when
I asked the man for the name of his father, I knew that he

had spoken the truth; so I said to him :—' O brave man !
Thou hast placed me under great obligations, and I am
bound to point out thy foe to thee, and to make an end of
thy search I inform thee that I am Ibrahim Ibn Sulaimân ;
avenge the blood of thy father upon me.'—He would not
believe me, and replied :—' Thou art weary of life, and
wishest to be delivered of thy misery.'—I rejoined :—' No,
by Allah ! I have slain him.' Then I gave him indica-
tions by which he knew that I had spoken the truth. Now
he changed colour, his eyes became bloodshot, and after
pausing a while he continued :—' It may quickly happen to
thee to join my father as he himself desires thee to do.
But arise, for fear I might nullify the safety I granted thee ;
and depart, for I cannot restrain myself, and might do
thee harm.'— After saying this he presented me with one
thousand dinârs, which I took, and went out."

Verses :

O brave man, learn thou bravery !
From men of the world learn manliness,
Preserve thy heart from the remorse of remorse-seekers,
Preserve thy tongue from the blame of evil-speakers,
Requite with good him who did thee evil
Because by that evil he injured his own prosperity.
If thou makest beneficence thy rule
The good thou doest will return only to thee.

STORY.

One night a great mosque in Egypt, having caught fire,
was burnt. The Musalmâns suspected that Christians had

committed the act, and in revenge put fire to·their houses, which consumed them. The Sultân of Egypt had the persons captured who burnt these houses, and having assembled them in one spot, ordered notes to be distributed among them, on some of which a sentence of death to the bearer was written, on some to cut off his hands, and on some to whip him. These notes having been thrown to the culprits and been picked up by them, each of them underwent the punishment which had fallen to his lot. One, to whom the sentence of death had been awarded, said :—"I do not fear to be killed, but I have a mother, of whom no one will take care except·myself." Near him stood a man who was to be punished by whipping, but they exchanged their notes, the latter saying:—"I have no mother, let me be killed instead of him, and him be whipped instead of me," and this was done.

Verses :

Liberality may be practiced with silver and gold.
Blessed is he who is liberal with his life ;
When he learnt that his friend needs his life
He sacrificed his own to save that of his friend.

STORY.

Asm'ayi says :—" I was acquainted with a liberal man whose house I constantly frequented for the purpose of enjoying his bounty. Once when I made my appearance at his door, the keeper of it prevented me from entering, and said :—'The reason of my not allowing thee to go in is distress and poverty.' Then I wrote the following [Arabic] distich :— '

Verses :

If a liberal man is [inaccessible] within a curtain
What is the superiority of a liberal man over a miser?

This I gave to the doorkeeper, who took it in, and after tarrying for a while, came out with the following written on its back :—

Arabic Distich.

If a liberal man possesses little
He hides himself within a curtain from his creditor.

This note was, however, accompanied by a purse of 500 dinârs, and I said to myself :—' Anything more strange than this has never occurred to me, and I shall carry this money as a present into the assembly of Mâmûn.'* When I entered, the Khalifah asked me whence I had come, and I replied : ' From the most liberal of Arabs.', He inquired who he is, and I said that he is a man who' had given me a share of his knowledge and of his wealth. Then I placed the said purse before him on the ground, but on perceiving it he turned pale and said :—' This is the seal of my treasurer, and I want to see that man.' I replied :—' O Amir, I would be ashamed to see him frightened by one of thy officials.' Then Mâmûn said to one of his courtiers :—' Go with Asm'ayi, and when thou seest that man, tell him that I

---

* The Khalifah Mâmûn reigned from the 20th March, 812, till the 30th July, 833.

summon him to my presence, but do so without disturbing his mind.' When the said man arrived, Mâmûn asked :— ' Art thou not the man who came to us yesterday pleading poverty and misery ; whereon we gave thee this purse to spend for thy food, and which thou hast given away for one distich sent to thee by Asm'ayi ?' He replied :—' By Allah, O Amir, in pleading poverty and misery I uttered no falsehood, but I would not send his messenger back except with what the Amir had sent me back.' Mâmûn being pleased with this explanation, ordered 1000 dinârs more to be given to him. Asm'ayi said :—' O Amir, make me also a sharer in this bounty with him.' Accordingly he ordered the gift to be completed by 1000 dinârs, and enrolled that man among his companions :—

Verses:

When the hand of a liberal man is without money
It is proper for him to close the door from poverty.
Yes, the shutting of the entrance is like
Tying up the mouth of the money bag."

STORY.

Hâtim* having been asked whether he had ever met with one more liberal than himself, replied :—" Yes, one day I alighted at the house of an orphan† who possessed ten sheep, but immediately slaughtered, cooked, and brought

---

* Hâtim Jâyi was an Arab who lived before the promulgation of Islâm, and was celebrated for his boundless liberality.

† The word is *Yatimi*, an orphan; but I suspect it to be an error for *Jamimi*, a man of the tribe of *Jamim*.

one for me. I was pleased with a particular piece of the meat, which I consumed, and said :—' By Allah, this is very savoury.'—The youth then went out, killed all his sheep, and taking from each that special portion of meat, cooked it, and brought it to me, without my suspecting it. When I went out to mount my horse, I saw a great quantity of blood spillèd outside the house, and on asking for the reason, was informed that he had slaughtered all his sheep. I blamed him, and asked why he had done so? but he replied :—' Allah be praised! As something which I possessed had pleased thee, it would have been accounted very bad manners on my part among the Arabs, if I had withheld it from thee.' " Hâtim being asked what he had given in return, replied :—" Three hundred red haired camels, and five hundred sheep ; " and, on being told that he was more liberal, he continued :—" Alas! He gave all he had, and I only a little of what I possess."

Verses :

When a mendicant who has but half a loaf
Gives it all away from his house
It is more than if the Shâh of the world
Gives away one half of his treasury.*

STORY.

A poet, expecting gain, presented himself several days in succession, at the house of Mo'an Zaid,† and not being able

---

* This is something like the widow's mite in the Gospel.
† The name of a man celebrated for his liberality.

to see him, went into his garden, the keeper of which he requested to let him know when Mo'an arrived, and took his seat near the water. At the proper time the gardener gave the required information to the poet, who then recited the following [Arabic] distich :—

Verses:

O for the liberality of Mo'an ! the crown with us [M'anâ] in my necessity
I have no intercessor for me with Mo'an but thyself.

Having written this distich upon a board, he threw it into the water, and when it reached Mo'an he ordered it to be taken out. When he had perused the writing, he called the poet, gave him a purse of gold, and put away the board under his carpet. The next day he pulled out the board, read the contents, summoned the poet to his presence and presented him with 100,000 dinârs; and on the third day he acted in the same manner. Now the poet became afraid that his benefactor might repent, and take back what he had given him ; accordingly he took flight. When on the fourth day Mo'an again drew forth the board and called for the poet, he could not be found, whereon Mo'an said :—" It was incumbent upon me in the duty of liberality, to continue the same towards him till not a dirhem remained in my treasury, but he entertained no such expectations."

Verses:

Who is liberal ? He who, when a mendicant brings
To his door as great hopes as his heart can hold,

Opens the hand of bounty and gives him so much,
That it surpasses the expectations of the asker.

STORY.

An Arab of the desert welcomed the arrival of an Arab chief in a Qasidah recited by him, which terminated in the following [Arabic] distich :—

Verses:

Stretch out thy hand to me, the palm whereof
Distributes largesses, and its back is kissed.

Accordingly the generous man held out his hand to be kissed by the Arab, whereon he said by way of a joke :— "The hairs upon thy lips have scratched my hand." The Arab replied :—" What injury can the bristles of a porcupine inflict upon the paw of a formidable lion ? " This sally pleased the liberal man, who said :—" I like this better than the Qasidah," and ordered him to be rewarded for it with 1000 and for the sally 3000 dirhems ;—

Verses :

Who exaltes thy head with praise above the skies
Is meaner than anyone else, if he be not skilled in words.
Consider him to be skilled in words who discerns
Bad from good, and good expressions from better ones.

FIFTH GARDEN

Record of the tender state of nightingales of the meadow of love and affection, and the fluttering of the wings of butterflies of the congregations of desire and friendship.

It is quoted in tradition as a saying of the prophet that "He who loves, remains chaste, restrains his passion, and dies, has died a martyr." The merit of chastity and restraint consists in bridling the lusts of physical nature, which, if indulged in, manifest themselves as animal passions and not as the excellencies of the human soul :—

Verses :

That love, which is one of the special virtues of man,
Must wherever it arises, be kept chaste and restrained.
The love which follows nature and sensual appetite
Is a quality of the natures of animals and beasts of prey.

STORY.

Two intelligent men were conversing about love. One of them said :—"Trouble and pain are peculiarities of love ; a lover is at all times enduring trouble and suffering distress." The other replied :—" Hush ! Hast thou never seen reconciliation after quarrel, or never tasted the joy of union after separation? None in the world are more agreeable than those who cultivate love with pure hearts, and more coarse than stolid persons who never felt its charms."

Verses:

Beauty is [only] a ray of the mistress's love. When will a
    man's heart
Be attracted by the beauty of one whose heart is not affec-
    tionate?
Should an ignorant man ask for a reason of this law
A sufficient one is, that kindred natures sympathise.

STORY.

During the time of his own Khalifate, Sadig Akbar* (may Allah be pleased with him) was walking about in the lanes of Madinah, and happened to pass near a house from which he heard sounds of lamentation, and beheld a woman reciting the following distichs, whilst hot tears fell from her eyes :—

Verses:

O thy stature is in beauty more excellent than the moon
In comparison to the stature of thy moon the sun is inferior;
Before the nurse places milk upon my lips
I drink blood in memory of thy red lips.

The hearing of these distichs made such an impression on Sadig that he knocked at the door, and the speaker having come out frightened, he asked her whether she was free or

---

* Sadig Akbar is the epithet of Abu Bakar, the immediate successor of the prophet ; he reigned from A.H. 11 till 14 (A.D. 632 till 34).

a slave, and she said that she was a bondsmaid. He further asked for the love of whom she had recited the verses, and for whom she had shed tears? She replied:—" O Khalifah, I adjure thee by the soul of the prophet, and by his illuminated mausoleum, to let me alone." He continued: "I shall not move a step till I have elicited the secret of thy heart." The girl then heaved a deep sigh, and mentioned the name of a youth of the Beni Hâshem. Sadig (may Allah be pleased with him) then went to the mosque, called for the owner of that slave-girl, purchased her, gave the price to the owner, and sent her to her lover.

Verses :

O heart, who knows how to unite thee to the love of thy
　desire
But He who is exempt from all vicissitudes of time?
Thou wilt succeed by suffering, but if thou canst not,
Then lament that the hearts of compassionate persons may
　be moved.

STORY.

A songstress, celebrated for her pleasing voice, her graceful melodies, as well as her other incomparable charms and spotless beauty, was one day performing for her owner in a balcony, and engaged in singing, whilst a youth, standing beneath, with his heart enamoured, and his mind restless, listened to her voice, which calmed him, and the sweetness of the melody fascinated him.

Verses :

The lover deprived of the sight of his mistress is happy
If he　n but listen to her speech in the rear of a wall.

Putting out his head suddenly from the balcony, the owner perceived the young man, gave him a seat at his own table, and conversed with him on various subjects. The youth, whilst paying attention with his mind to the owner, fixed his eyes upon the girl, and replied to whatever she asked, by her glances, with his brows; and whatever knots she tied with her ringlets, he solved by his sweet smiles.

Verses:

What is more pleasant than the meeting of two lovers,
Agreeing with each other in spite of their foes,
Dallying together with their eyes and brows,
Seeking an opportunity to embrace and to kiss.

After the entertainment, the owner, being obliged to absent himself, left the two anxious and ardent lovers to themselves. Then the girl sang the following two couplets to the youth :

Verses :

By God, who openly and secretly
Is worshipped by men and fairies,
I swear that of all whom I see in the world
No one is dearer to me than thou.

The youth listened to the strophes, uttered an exclamation, and said :—

Verses :

O thou who sawest me, and residest in my heart,
Soul and body, all now belong to thee,
If my heart inclines to thee it is no wonder,
It must be a stone, not a heart, which turns not to thee !

The girl said that now her only wish in the world was

that they should put their hands round each other's waists, and eat sugar from the lips of each other. The youth replied :—" My desire is the same, but what can I do ? as God the Most High says :—' The intimate friends on that day shall be enemies unto one another, except the pious,'* which means that on the day of resurrection friendship of friends will become enmity, except the friendship of the abstemious, which will increase the attachment. I do not wish that on the morn of resurrection the edifice of our love be impaired, and our friendship be turned into. enmity." After saying these words, he departed, reciting the following :—

Verses :

O heart, abandon this love of two days
Because a love of two days profits not,
Choose a love wherewith on the day of reckoning
Thou mayest abide in the eternal abode.

STORY.

A learned man says :—" Once I held an assembly and was sowing the seeds of [good] desires in the soil of the hearts of my hearers. An old man who was present and attentive, constantly sighed, but also shed tears without intermission. Having afterwards one day been asked by me for the reason, he said :—' I was a man who bought and sold slave boys and girls, gaining my livelihood by this

---

* Qurân, ch. xliii., v. 67.

trade. One day I had purchased for 300 dinârs a very beautiful boy :—.

Verses :

His lips were like fresh sugar, his cheeks like the shining moon.

His sugar had not yet been wiped by the nurse from milk.

I took much trouble to teach him, till he learnt the art of coquetry and dalliance. Then I took him like a second Joseph,* to the bâzâr, offered him for sale, enumerating his qualities and attractions ; all of a sudden I beheld a very handsome young man, dressed according to the fashion of devotees, who had arrived on horseback, and perceiving the slave-boy from the corner of his eye, alighted. He approached him and asked him, what country he had come from, what trade he knew, and what work he could do ? Then turning to me he asked his price. I replied :—" Although in beauty and attractions he is only one dinâr, his price is one thousand of full weight." He said nothing, but taking hold of the boy's hand, unperceived by the other persons present, he slipped something into it. When the man had gone away, I weighed what he had given to the boy, and found it to be 100 dinârs. On the second and third days he acted in the same manner, so that the sum total he had presented to the boy amounted to 300 dinârs. I then said to myself :—He has paid the full price for the boy, is at-

---

* The biblical Joseph is meant, who was a paragon of beauty, according to Moslem tradition.

G

tached to him and unable to give the price I fixed. Accordingly I hastened after him, found his house, and when the
night had set in, I arose, adorned the boy with nice garments, perfumed him with pleasant odours, took him to the
house of the said young man, knocked at his door, which
he opened, but was confused on beholding us, and said :—
" We belong to Allah, and unto him shall we surely return."*
He asked who had brought us, and who had shown us the
way ? I replied :—"Some sons of noblemen haggled for
the boy but no sale was effected, and fearing that during
the night an attempt might be made to kidnap him, I now
bring him to spend this night under thy protection." He
said :—" Come thou in, and also remain with him." I
replied that I had some business to attend to, and would
therefore be unable to comply. Accordingly I left the boy
with him, went away, reached my house, closed the door, sat
down, and considered how they would spend the night, and
on what terms their companionship would be established,
when I heard all of a sudden, the voice of the boy who had
arrived trembling and weeping. I asked what had happened
to him in the company of the said young man that he
arrived in this condition ? The slave boy replied :—" That
noble fellow has died and surrendered his soul to his
creator." I said :—" Praise be to Allah, how was that ? "
He continued :—" When thou hadst gone home, he took
me to the interior of the house and brought me food. When

---

* Qurân, ch. ii., v, 151.

I had eaten and washed my hands, he spread out a bed for me, sprinkled musk and rosewater upon me, laid me down, and stroking my face, said :—' Praise be to Allah, how good and how beloved, but how unpleasant is what my soul lusts for, and the punishment of God the Most High is the most grievous of all, since he whom it befalls, is the most unfortunate of all men.' Then he uttered the words :—' Verily we belong to Allah, and verily to Him we return,' and continued :—' I bear witness that this is great beauty, but chastity and purity are more beautiful, as well as the reward promised for them, which is the most perfect of all.'—Then he fell down, and when I shook him I found that he was dead and had departed to eternal life."

The old man said :—" All my weeping is in remembrance of that young man, whose chastity, purity, and grace I can never forget, and whose other good qualities are always before my eyes. Whilst I live I shall follow his ways, and when I die it will be in that manner.

Verses :

As that friend of mine departed, who is better than the whole world;

I shall bemoan his loss more than the whole world,

My heart now sheds tears of blood, from my pale cheek to the ground,

When I depart under ground, I still shall weep in this manner.

STORY.

A youth, Salil by name, of noble lineage, and known

among the Arab tribes by his beauty and urbanity, but also
celebrated for his bravery in lion-hunting and prowess on
the battlefield, had fallen in love with a daughter of his
uncle, whom he succeeded in wedding after overcoming
great obstacles. He had, however, scarcely begun to enjoy
his felicity, and had not quaffed more than one drop from
the bowl of union, when he determined to take up his abode
in another locality, and having placed his wife in a litter,
started on his journey. After travelling one stage, Salil
reached a pleasant spot, where he caused the litter to be
deposited. He, however, suddenly caught sight of thirty
horsemen, whereon he snatched up his arms and galloping
to meet them, soon discovered that they were foes who had
come in pursuit of him, and an encounter having taken
place, he killed several of them, but was also himself
wounded, and returning to his uncle's daughter said :—

Verses :

I know that my foes desire to slay me
—Be seated that I may have a sad look at thee—
Then to shed thy blood, as they will shed mine,
So that no one else may touch thy lips.

The girl said :—" By Allah ! If thou wilt not shed my
blood, I shall do so myself, and commingle it with thine ;
but it will be better for thee to forestall me, and so relieve
my heart by the act." Then Salil arose and said :—

Verses :

By the unfair wrestling of this world
Look how I am prostrated to the dust !

She for whom I would fain sacrifice my life
Must this day be slain by my hand !

Then shedding a flood of tears, he drew his scimitar and with one stroke extinguished that world-illuminating lamp, and smearing his face with the blood of his spouse, he again rushed at his foes, several of whom he slew, fighting till at last he also himself succumbed. When the people of Salil became aware of what had taken place, they hastened with great lamentations to the spot, conveyed the two corpses to the cemetery of the tribe, and buried them in one grave.

Verses :

They put both with honours under ground
That they may not arise in sorrow and shame on the day of
    requital ;
They made a place of one kind in the hollow of the earth
That they may pleasantly sleep together, and arise together.

STORY.

A perfectly well-mannered youth, Ashter by name, had fallen in love with a beautiful maiden connected with the chiefs of the tribe. Her name was Habzâ, and the bonds of love and union having been firmly established between them, they kept their affection sec·et from friends and strangers, striving as much as possibl:· to prevent its becoming known.

Verses:

Love is a secret which cannot be revealed,
But by two hundred curtains it cannot be concealed.

At last their secret became divulged, and after being discussed in public, brought on quarrels between the two
families, so that bloodshed ensued, whereon the people of
Habzâ struck their tents and migrated to another district.
After a protracted separation, Ashter, being no longer able
to bear it, asked a friend to accompany him to the place
where his mistress dwelt, and to aid him to meet her, because from longing for her, his soul had risen to his lips,
and his days had been changed into nights. His friend
replied :—" To hear is to obey ; I shall do as thou listest,
and comply with thy behests." Accordingly both mounted
their camels, and in twenty-four hours reached the locality
near which the people of his mistress were encamped, and
alighted in a hollow near a mountain in the vicinity. Ashter
said to his friend :—" Arise, and betake thyself to that tribe
as a spy, mention no names to any one, but search for a
certain girl who takes care of the sheep and is an intimate
friend of Habzâ. Salute her, ask her about Habzâ, and
show her the spot where I am." The young man went on
his errand, the result of which he narrated as follows :—" I
arose, approached the tribe, and the first person I met was
the said shepherdess, to whom I conveyed the greetings of
Ashter, and asked for news about Habzâ. She replied :—
' Her husband keeps her in close confinement, and takes
great care of her, but those trees will be your place of meeting, and you must be there at the time of night prayers.'—I
returned, informed Ashter, and we [two friends] slowly
proceeded with our camels to the spot pointed out, which
we reached at the appointed time.

Verses :

We waited with tears and sighs,
Sitting on the path of the friend, when suddenly
The voice of ornaments and anklets was heard
Saying :—" Arise I The young lady has arrived."*

Ashter leapt forward, saluted the girl, and kissed her hand;
I turned away from them and went in another direction, but
they recalled me, saying :—" Come back, there is nothing
improper, and our intention is only to converse." Accordingly I joined them again ; they spoke about the past and
the future with each other, till at last Ashter said :—" I
hope thou wilt remain with me this night, and not scratch
the face of my expectations with the nail of separation."
Habzâ replied :—" By Allah I This wish cannot be gratified,
and nothing is more difficult to me than to assent to it.
Dost thou want past events to be repeated, and the doors of
calamity again to be opened ?" Ashter rejoined :—" By
Allah I I shall not abandon thee, nor take off my hands
from thy skirt."

Hemistich :

Let come what may, let happen what may !

Habzâ then asked :—" Will this friend of thine have the
courage to do what I bid him ?" I arose, and said :—" I
shall do whatever thou listest, even at the risk of my life."
Then she undressed herself, and said :—" Put on these

---

* The expression ; *The Moon of fourteen has arrived*, would be awkward in English, and has been rendered as shown above.

garments, and give thine to me. Enter my tent and sit
down behind the curtain. My husband will come with a
bowl of milk and will say :—' This is thy drink, take it.'—
Be not hasty but delay a little to take the goblet, whereon
he will either give it to thee with his own hand, or deposit
it on the ground ; he will then go away and not return till
next morning.' I followed all her instructions, but when
her husband brought the milk, I stretched forth my hand to
take hold of the bowl whilst he was in the act of putting it
on the ground, so that I accidently struck the vessel and
spilled the milk, whereat he became angry, saying :—" Wilt
thou insult me ? " and brought forth a dreadful whip of
twisted leather :—

Verses:

In thickness like a snake,
In length similar to a dragon ;
Painting a serpent was its task,
The surface for the painting a naked body.

He bared my back, struck it vigorously, like a drum on the
day of battle. I had neither courage to shout, because I
feared he would know me by my voice ; nor to bear
patiently the tearing of my skin, and intended to leap up
and cut off his head with a sword, but reflecting that this
would raise a tumult which nobody could quell, I remained
quiet, till the mother and sister of Habzâ became aware of
what he was doing, and liberating me from his grasp, took
me away. I turned my back towards them, wrapped myself up, and moaned, whereon the woman said :—" O my

daughter! Fear God, and do not act contrary to the wishes of thy husband, because one hair of his head is more precious than a thousand Ashters; in fact, who is he that thou shouldst for his sake endure trouble and castigation ? " Then she arose, saying :—" I shall send thy sister to keep thee company this night," and went away. After a while the sister of Habzâ made her appearance, weeping and cursing the man who had whipped me. I replied nothing, and she laid herself down by my side. When she had become quiet, I stretched out my hand, and, putting it on her mouth, said :—" Thy sister is with Ashter, and I have suffered this misery instead of her. Keep this secret, or else we shall both be disgraced." She was first in a state of astonishment, which was however, gradually changed to one of familiarity, so that she was chatting and laughing till dawn. When it was morning, Habzâ arrived, who became frightened on beholding us, and asked :—" Woe to thee ! Who is this by thy side ? " I told her that it was her own sister, and on her making further enquiries I told her that time was precious, and she must ask her own sister. Then I took my garments, joined Ashter, and departed. Whilst travelling I informed him of what had taken place ; he examined my back, saw the wounds made by the flagellation, condoled with me, and said that philosophers had recorded the maxim :—" A friend in need, is a friend indeed, because there is no want of friends in prosperity."

Verses :

O heart, when a time of sorrow overtakes thee
There will be no sorrow if thou hast a kind friend ;

For a day of trouble a friend is required,
Because in times of comfort, friends are not scarce.

STORY.

Once when Rashid* arrived in Kufah, his vazir had gone
to the slave-market where a youth, said to possess great
accomplishments, was offered to him, and reporting this to
Rashid he was ordered to purchase him. At the time of
departure, the youth was heard weeping and singing :—

Verses :

Who sheds my guiltless blood by separating me from my
    friend
Ought to spare the blood of one distressed like me.
If one day of separation has brought me such despair
Alas, what will be my state when a month and year elapse.

This having been brought to the notice of Rashid, he summoned him to his presence, and elicited from him that he
was in love with some one in Kufah ; whereon Rashid took
pity and emancipated him. The vazir said :—" It is a pity
to liberate a fellow who has such a beautiful voice," but
Rashid answered :—" It would be a pity to retain in slavery
a man with such noble feelings."

Verses:

O thou, who desirest to enjoy royal dignity
And hast the power to manumit slaves

---

* The celebrated Khalifah Harûn-al-Rashid is meant, who reigned
A. D. 786—809.

Liberate him who is a slave to love
Because bondage of love is enough for him who lost his
   heart.

STORY.

A beautiful woman had many admirers, whose attentions
were so assiduous that the very street in which she lived
became thronged by her visitors, but when her attractions
disappeared and she had become ugly, her lovers abandoned
her.   Then I said to one of them :—" She is the same
friend as before, with the same eyes, brows, lips, but perhaps
her stature is more tall and her body more stout.   It is
faithless and treacherous on thy part to neglect her."   He
replied :—" Alas, for what thou sayest !   That which ravished
the heart, and enthralled the senses, was the spirit which
resided in her form, in the gracefulness of her limbs, the
smoothness of her skin, and in the pleasantness of her voice,
but as that spirit has departed from the figure, how can I
love a dead body, or fondle a withered rose ? "

Verses :

The rose has left the garden, of what use are the thorns?
The Shâh is not in the town, of what use is his retinue ?
Belles are the cage, beauty and attraction the parrot
When the parrot has fled, of what use is the cage ?

STORY.

A belle, whose beauty and attractions had disappeared,
and whose face was getting hirsute, found that those who
formerly liked her society, now kept away, and that her
lovers were disgusted, because hairs were growing around

her chin like an irregular net, which scared away the birds of their hearts. Accordingly, she summoned a barber, telling him that she had become dismayed because she had no friend nor any one to purchase her favours, requesting him to remove that veil and to tear up that net. The barber who was a wit, and of genial temper, said :—

Verses :

When a beardless youth's term of beauty has set in
He ought for coquetry to shave his chin and ear-tips,
But when the cheek has become rough by the operation
It will be like wood, scratching the surface of the heart.

Nuktah.

An amorous fellow who was distressed by the modesty of the boy whom he loved, and feared the incivility of his guardian, said to himself :—"When will the beard sprout on that smooth face, and the conceit of beauty depart from that head, that I may freely offer my services, and take rest in his society without ceremony." I have heard that when the hope of that man was fulfilled, and the freshness of that boy's beauty had come to an end, he also like others, kept aloof, and no longer wished to enjoy the sight of the boy. Being twitted for his fickleness, he replied :—" What did I know that this bird would soar into the air, and that this this captivity will be snapped by a hair ? "

Verses :

I read in books that a beard is a wing,
According to the opinions of learned men ;

But a wing whereby to the land of non-existence
The bird of innocence takes flight.

Verses :

The gloss of thy beauty is gone, O boy,
Expect not verdure from a withered plant,
Thy verdant down is now turning black,
Wash out beauty's conceit from thy heart.
The few hairs now sprouting on thy chin
Are like those of old men with but few hairs.

STORY.

A Darwêsh, being madly in love with a dissolute woman, was running about, shed tears, and heaved sighs, but could never extort a glance of compassion from her. Being told that his mistress always associated with intoxicated men, slept with wine-bibbers, and was not a friend to Darwêshes, wherefore it would be better to keep aloof from her, since she required companions similar to herself, and to mind his own business ; the Darwêsh after listening to this advice smiled, and said :—

Verses :

My portion is the pain of love, and I shall not
Blame my mistress if another is captivated by her charms;
She is a rosegarden of beauty, and no wonder
If a thistle-gatherer plucks briars, and a rose-fa——ier roses.

STORY.

A handsome youth was by the lasso of d' re attracted to

a ring of Darwêshes, and he reposed like a centre in the circle of Sûfis.

Verses :

He became a reflection of the Qiblah.* Those who seek God
Turned their countenances from God towards him.
Those who wear the habit of religion, crowded
Around the sweet-spoken boy like flies around sugar.

Every one desired to possess him all to himself, and tried to make himself agreeable to him, so that at last this rivalry produced dissension among them, and they quarrelled :—

Verses :

Amorous fellows are prone to fall out with each other
When all of them avow their love to one mistress.
When ardor excites those who go round the K'abah†
It is likely that they will clash against each other.

The superior‡ of the monastery, whose cap was made of the same felt, and whose analogous pretensions bore every moment witness against him, called the boy and advised him, saying :—" O beloved son, and amiable youth ; do not commingle with every one, like milk and sugar, and do not fall into the deceitful snares of every wretch. Thou art

---

* Quiblah i he direction towards K'abah or Temple of Mekkah, in which Moslem. 'lways turn when they are praying.
† It is one ea the religious ordinances that the pilgrims must also walk, or rather , round the K'abah when they perform the Hajj.
‡ The word is orc, "old man."

the God-showing mirror, and it would be a pity to be familiar with every heedless fellow."

Verses :

Do not every moment put thyself in the power of strangers,
Admit not general acquaintances to thy special intimacy.
Thy face is a mirror, which has been polished,
Do not allow rust to settle upon the bright mirror.

When the sweet boy had heard this advice, he became displeased, made a wry face, rose, and left the monastery on some pretext. He did not return for some days and the Murids* were extremely grieved at his departure, so that in their lamentations they bored with the diamonds of their eye-lashes the jewels of weakness and misery,† apologising as follows :—

Verses :

Return, no one has power over thee, O boy,
Sit with whom thou choosest, and neglect whom thou wilt.

Quatrain :—

Although thou deceivest the intellect and art a foe to
    religion
Return, because thou art a consolation to a broken heart,
It is unfortunate, distressing, and miserable for us
To know thee sitting with others as an uninvited guest.

That youth accepted their excuses, abandoned his cold-

---

* The disciples of the *Pir*.
† This simply means that *they wept*, the lashes being the diamond-points which bored through the pearls of the tears, here called jewels of misery.

ness and returned to the society of those whom he had
abandoned, and who had been pained by his absence.

Verses :

After four things, the hope of four others

Is better, such as repose and mercy after punishment,

Union after separation, fidelity after falsehood,

Peace after quarrelling, and reconciliation after blame.

SIXTH GARDEN

Blowing of the zephirs of wit, and the breezes of jocular
sallies, which cause the buds of the lips to laugh and
the flowers of the hearts to bloom.

There is a tradition that the lord of apostleship (may the benediction of Allah be upon him, and upon his family, and peace) has said :—" A true believer is fond of jokes, and is of pleasant speech, but a hypoctite is ill-humoured."* 'Ali the prince of the Faithful (may Allah reward him, and ennoble his face), said :—" There is no harm in any one joking so as to get rid of a bad temper, and a sour face." The apostle (Benediction from Allah and peace be upon him), said to a hag, that old women do not enter paradise ; whereon she wept, and he continued :—" Because God the Most High causes them to arise more young and beautiful than they were, and takes them to paradise." He once said to a woman of the Anssâr :—" Ask thy husband ! There is whiteness in his eyes !" She quickly went, and in great confusion repeated the words of the prophet. Her husband

---

* Literally, " has a sour face."

replied :—" That is true enough, there is whiteness and also blackness in my eyes, but not for the worse."

Verses :

If a contented man jokes, blame him not,
It is a trade licit by the laws of reason and religion ;
The heart is a mirror, and vexation the rust on it,
That rust is best polished away by jocularity.

PLEASANTRY.

One day, Asm'ayi being present at the table of Hârûn, *Pâlûdah** was brought in, whereon Asm'ayi said that there were many Arabs who had never seen *Pâlûdah* nor heard the name of it. Hârûn replied :—" Bring a witness to prove the truth of what thou hast asserted, or else it is a lie." Afterwards Hârûn went one day to hunt, and Asm'ayi was with him. An Arab happened to be coming empty from the desert. Hârûn desired Asm'ayi to bring him ; the latter accordingly went and said to the Arab :—" The Amir of the Faithful wants thee ; obey."—" Have the Faithful an Amir ? "—" Yes."—" I have no Faith in him."— Then Asm'ayi reproved him and said :—" O son of an adulteress, why dost thou speak thus ? " The Arab likewise getting angry, took hold of Asm'ayi's collar, pulled him about, and insulted him, whilst Hârûn, who witnessed the scene from a distance, laughed. At last Asm'ayi succeeded in pulling the Arab to Hârûn, and the Arab said :—" O Amir of the

---

* A kind of fluid dish, made of sherbert, honey, flour, and other in-gredients.

Faithful, as this man imagines; give me justice against him, for he has insulted me." Hârûn said :—"Give him two dirhems." The Arab continued :—"Praised be Allah ! He has insulted me, he must give me two dirhems more." Hârûn said :—" Let it be so, this is our command." Now the Arab turned to Asm'ayi and said : — "O son of two adulteresses, be quick, and give me four dirhems by order of the Amir."—Hârûn fell on his back from laughing, and made the Arab come with him, who, when they reached the castle, and when he saw all its pomp, was so struck by the surroundings of Hârûn, that he considered him to be a great man, and exclaimed :—"Salutation to thee, O prophet of Allah." He replied —" Hush ! What dost thou say ? " but the Arab continued :—"Salutation to thee, O apostle of Allah ! " On being again reproved and told that Hârûn was the Amir of the Faithful, he said :—"Salutation to thee, O Amir of the Faithful." Hârûn then said :—"Salutation to thee," and made him sit down. The table having been laid out, the Arab ate of everything, and when at last also *Pâlûdah* was brought, Asm'ayi said :—" I hope he does not know what *Pâlûdah* is." Hârûn replied :—" If the case be such I shall give thee a purse of gold." After that the Arab stretched forth his hand to eat *Pâlûdah*, but from the way he set about, it appeared that he had never before partaken of any. Accordingly Hârûn asked :—" What is it thou art eating ? " He replied :—" I swear by God, who has honoured thee with the Khalifship, that I do not know what this thing is, but God the Most High says in the glorious Qurân, *fruits*

*and palm-trees and pomegranates.** Palm-trees are near us, and
I am of opinion that these are pomegranates." Asm'ayi
said :—" O Amir ! Give me two purses, because as this
fellow does not know what Pâlûdah means, he is equally
ignorant of what pomegranates are." Accordingly Hârûn
ordered Asm'ayi to be presented with two purses, and the
Arab likewise, so that he became rich :—

Verses :

Knowest thou who is liberal ? He
Whose treasury knows no closing.
Whatever serious or funny comes before him
Is all made an occasion for his liberality.

PLEASANTRY.

One day the Khalifah took his meal, and, a roast lamb
having been placed before him, he called an Arab, who had
just arrived from the desert, to partake of it. The Arab at
once began to attack the whole body of the lamb, whereon
the Khalifah said :—" Thou art tearing up this lamb and
eating it with such relish, that it seems, its mother had
butted against thee with her head ? " The Arab replied :—
" This means eating ! But thou lookest so kindly, and
eatest so daintily, that it seems her mother had suckled
thee."

Verses :

A gentleman is so merciful and kind to his property
That he looks with a compassionate eye on everything.

---

* Qurân, ch. LV., v. 68.

If his lambs and sheep encounter some little danger
He ransoms them with his mother and beloved children.

Verses :

If, for instance, a gentleman lays out bread and a roasted lamb
Before thee on the table, if thou art one of his guests,
If thou makest a notch in his teeth with the stone of violence
It is better than that thy teeth make a notch in his bread,
If he receives from thy hand a hundred wounds on side and back
It is better than that thou shouldst fill thy emptiness with his roast.

PLEASANTRY.

When Bahlûl was asked to take the census of the fools of Bosrah, he replied that their number exceeded the bounds of calculation, but that if he were told to count the wise men, he would do so, because they were few :—

Verses :

Whatever sage thou mayest behold, he takes a share
Of some cash from the capital of folly in due season,
He lives unscorched by the sun of calamities
Comfortably under the shadow of folly.

PLEASANTRY.

A scholar was one day writing a letter to a frien⸗, and a man sitting by his side read from the corner of his eye what had been written. Being displeased with this trick, he

wrote :—" Had not a thief been sitting near me, and read-
ing what I wrote, I would have informed thee of all my
secrets," hereon the man exclaimed :—" By Allah ! O Mullânâ, I have not seen nor read thy letter." He replied :—
" O ignorant man ! Then tell me where thou hast taken
the words thou speakest ? "

Verses :

Who learns a man's secret by stealth
Must certainly be called a thief ;
The person who indulges in such tricks
Is to be called a female, not a man.

PLEASANTRY.

A drunken man coming out from a house fell to the
ground, soiling with dust his lips and mouth, which a dog
began to lick. The drunkard, imagining that it was a man
who had taken the trouble to clean him, prayed :—" May
God the Most High cause thy children to be thy servants."
The dog then raised his leg, and urinated on the drunkard,
who continued :—" May Allah bless thee, my lord, for
having brought warm water to wash my face."

Verses :

When a wine-bibber thinks it allowable
To get his whiskers soiled with dirty vomit,
. is proper for a dog to furnish warm urine
.om its bladder to wash his dirty whiskers.

PLEASANTRY.

The Qâzi of Baghdâd, having gone out on foot to pay a

visit to the Friday-mosque, encountered a drunken man who recognised him, and said :—" May Allah honour thee, O Qâzi ! Is it admissible that thou shouldst walk on foot ?" Then he swore that he would bear the Qâzi on his neck, and the latter said :—" Come near thou accursed fellow." After he had mounted on the drunkard's back, the latter asked :—" Am I to trot sharply or gently ?" The Qâzi said :—" Between the one and the other, but thou must neither run away nor stumble, and keep close to the walls of the houses, so that I may be safe from being knocked against those who are walking on the road." The man said :— " Allah bless thee, O Qâzi, how well thou knowest the rules of equitation ! " When he had carried the Qâzi to the mosque, the latter ordered him to be thrown into prison, whereon he exclaimed :—" May Allah correct thee, O Qâzi ! Is this the reward of him who has saved thee from the disgrace of walking, has become thy horse, and has conveyed thee with dignity to the mosque ? " The Qâzi laughed and left him alone.

Verses :

If a drunkard mars thy path and wants to quarrel
Deal kindly with him, O wise man of business.
The intention of an intelligent experienced man is like a
    hair,
Suffer not the wrangling of silly persons to break it in
    twain.

Pleasantry.

A weaver, who had left something in trust with a learned man, desired again to have it back some time afterwards, and going to ask for it, he saw the man sitting in front of his house on the professorial couch, with a number of his disciples in front of him. He said :—" Mullânâ ! I am in need of my deposit." He replied :—" Wait an hour till I finish my lecture." The weaver accordingly took a seat, and, as the lecture proceeded, he observed that the Mullânâ often shook his head ; and thinking that the imparting of the lesson consisted in this, he said :—" O professor ! Arise and let me take thy place till thy return, and wag my head till thou hast brought out my deposit, because I am in haste." On hearing these words the learned man said :—

Verses:

The lawyer of the town is boasting in a general assembly
That he knows the revealed and occult part of sciences,
But the answer to whatever thou mayest ask,
Is a motion of the hand, or wagging of the head.

PLEASANTRY.

A blind man walked in the night, holding a lamp, and carrying a jar on his back. A captious fellow who met him said :—" O ignorant man ! Day and night are the same to thee, and so are light and darkness to thy eyes ; then what is the use of this lamp ?" The blind man replied, laughing :—" This lamp is not for me, but for thyself, who art blind at heart and heedless, that thou mayest not knock against me and break my jar."

Verses:

No man knows the state of an ignoramus better than an
  ignoramus,

Although he [the critic] may be more learned than Avicenna.*

Reprove not a blind man, O thou who boastest of sight,
Because one who cannot see has sight in his own affairs.

PLEASANTRY.

'Amru Leith saw one of his troopers mounted on a weak horse :—

Verses :

This weak little horse which has not obtained
Substance except from bones, and composition by symmetry :
Its bones are shrunk like those of Ozair's ass,†
But no flesh has yet grown upon the bones.

Verses :

A lean horse ! So that if thou seekest
Thou wilt not find a particle of flesh on him,
If thou diggest him out from head to heel
Thou wilt find nothing except skin and bone.

He said :—" Alas for my soldiers ! Every dinâr and dirhem I gave them they spent to fatten the wombs of women, and they have melted their horses by starvation."

---

* The Arabic and full name of Avicenna, whose Europeanised form I used above, and who was born in the vicinity of Bokhara, A.H. 370 (A.D. 980), is as follows :—'Abu 'Ali Husain Ibn 'Abdullah Ibn Sina.—In our text above the abridged form Abu 'Ali Sina is used.

† 'Ozair is supposed to have been the Ezra of the Bible. The bones of his ass were raised and clothed with flesh, and the animal became alive again.—See *D'Herbelot. Bibliothèque Orientale*, article *Ozair.*

The man, bearing these words, replied :— "By Allah, O Amir! If thou wilt cast a scrutinising glance upon the womb of my wife, thou wilt see that it is more lean than the posterior of my horse." 'Amru Leith smiled, gave him a large present, and said :—"Go and fatten both thy vehicles !"

Verses :

God gave thee two vehicles ; place thy burden
Sometimes upon the one, sometimes upon the other,
Take off the burden from one in the night, from the other
     in the day,
Put one of them under the saddle, the other under the
     thigh.

PLEASANTRY.

A descendant of 'Ali called a woman, but she asked him for dinârs and dirhems, whereon he said :—"Art thou not satisfied that a member of the family of prophetship and the house of vicarship* has connection with thee?"— She replied :—"Tell this fable to the courtezans of Kulshânah, but do not seek to gratify that wish with the courtezans of Baghdad, except by means of dinârs and dirhems."

Verses :

Unless thou give to a fool double of what thou wantest from
     him
Hope not that he will gratify thy wish.

---

* Muhammad being the prophet, and 'Ali the vicar of Allah.

Open the knot of thy purse, because a courtezan
Unties not her trousers for the love of God or the prophet.

PLEASANTRY.

A learned man, of ugly figure and hideous aspect, paid a
visit to Farazdaq,* and observing that his face had become
yellow from disease, said :—"What was the matter with
thee that thy countenance has become so yellow ? " He
replied :—" When I beheld thee, I bethought myself of my
sins, and my complexion changed to this colour." He
continued :—" Why hast thou remembered thy transgres-
sions ? " Farazdaq replied :—"Because I feared God the
Most High would punish me and metamorphose me into a
figure like thine."

Verses :

When my heart beholds thy ugly cheek
It reveals the knots of long kept secrets,
Wherefore I dread that for my base sins
The wrath of God may transform me, like thee.

PLEASANTRY.

The same learned man says :—" I stood with a friend on
a road, conversing with him, when a woman halted opposite
to me, looking at me steadfastly. When this staring had
passed all bounds, I despatched my slave to ask the woman
what she was listening to. He came back and reported
that the woman had said :—' My eyes had committed a

---

* There was also a man of this name, known for his beneficence, who
lived before the time of Islâm.

great sin; I intended to inflict a punishment upon them, and could devise none worse than looking at that hideous face : ' "—

Verses :

The leaven of sin could not be washed out from the pupils
    of my eyes
Although I wept twice hundred times over a fire ;
But to be saved from the fire of the resurrection, I to-day
Punished them by contemplating thy hideous face.

PLEASANTRY.

The same learned man says :—" I never was so ashamed as on the day when a woman caught hold of my hand, and took me to the shop of a brass-founder. I was astonished, and asked him for the reason, whereon he said :—" She had told me to make a figure of Satan for her, and on my telling her that I did not know in what form, she pointed to thee, saying :—' According to this figure.' "

Verses :

Thou hast indeed a wonderful form,
No one can make a form like this ;
To portray Satan's countenance
Thy face alone can as a model serve.

PLEASANTRY.

A man heard another, who was very ugly, praying for the pardon of his sins, and asking for deliverance from the fire of hell ; whereon he said :—" O my friend, why art thou shy

of hell, with such a face, and wishest to save it from the fire
of it ! "

Verses :

As thou canst not see thy face
It is unpleasant to others ; not to thee,
If therewith thou art into fire cast
The fire is to be pitied, and not thou.

PLEASANTRY.

A man with an ugly face paid a visit to a physician, and
said :—" I have a boil on the ugliest spot." The physician
looked into his face, and replied :—" Thou hast told me a
lie, for I have examined thy face and seen no boil."

Verses :

On account of ugliness the legislator has forbidden thee
To denude thy limbs beneath the waist ;
But, as thy face is ugliest of all, what wonder
Thou hast concealed it and bared another place.

PLEASANTRY.

A man with a large nose, who was courting a woman,
enumerated his virtues, and also said :—" I am a man far
from being light and giddy, able to bear a great deal, and
patient." She replied :—" If thou hadst not been able to
bear burdens with patience, thou wouldst surely not have
carried about this nose during forty years."

Verses :

Thy big nose is burdensome to all,
How long wilt thou absurdly shove it here and there ?

Thy constant prostration is not for worship's sake
But to place thy heavy nose's burden on the ground.

PLEASANTRY.

A wit saw a man with luxuriant hair on his face, and said :—" Pull out these hairs, for fear thy face will become thy head."

Verses :

If the gentleman fails to use the hair clipper
Daily upon the hirsute countenance
But few days will elapse when his face
Will, on account of the hair, pretend to be his head.

PLEASANTRY.

Mo'aviah* and 'Oqail Ben Abu Tâleb were sitting to-gether, when Mo'aviah said :—" O ye people of Syria, have you ever taken notice of the words of Allah the Most High, where He says :—*The hands of Abu Lahab shall perish and he shall perish.*† They said :—" Yes," and he continued : —" Abu Lahab is the uncle of 'Oqail." Then 'Oqail asked: —" O ye people of Syria, have you ever heard the words of Allah the Most High, where he says :—*'And his wife bearing wood.'*‡ They said " Yes," and he continued :—" She who bears the wood is the aunt of Mo'aviah."

---

* See footnote p. 49.
† Qurân, ch. CXI., v. 1.
‡ Ibidem, v. 4.

Verses :

If thou possessest knowledge of another man's fault
It is not the part of a wise man to explain it ;
He is silent about thee and thy faults, then why
Makest thou him speak of thy fault who is reticent ?

PLEASANTRY.

Quarrelling with a man, a descendant of 'Ali said to him
—" Thou considerest me as an enemy, whereas it is incumbent upon thee to implore a blessing upon me in every
prayer thou utterest, saying:—'O Allah ! Bless Muhammad and the family of Muhammad.'" The man replied :—
" I also add *those who are good and pure*, but thou art not
of them."

Verses :

O thou who reckonest thyself of the prophet's family
It will be testified so, by purity of character and qualities,
As thou claimest to be of those good men and women
It behoves thee also to possess their virtues.

PLEASANTRY.

An imposter, having adorned himself like a descendant of
'Ali, pretended to be one of that exalted family :—

Verses :

His claim was void of the evidence of truth
His very face and hair bore witness to the contrary.

He paid a visit to a generous man, who received him standing, and assigned to him the place of honour, sitting down

himself in the horse-shoe,* and bestowing upon him greater
presents than he expected.   When he departed, the highest
honours were again paid him, whereon some of the persons
present said :—'' We know this man, he is far from belong
ing to that family, and his claim is false, because neither his
father nor mother were in any way related to it : ''—

Verses :

His mother is a wandering mendicant in the town,
His father a mender of kettles, and carver of spindles ;
She belongs to the tribe of the low mob,
And he is but the grandson of a vagabond.

The generous man said :—'' What we have done was not
worthy of true members of that family, hut [only] suitable
for stray impostors : ''—

Verses :

Every one who has a share in the prophet's family
To honour him is not the privilege of every luckless man
    [like me],
He [the said impostor] is a stranger of the period, and if for
    his [the prophet's] love
One hazards his property and dignity, it is not strange.

PLEASANTRY.

A Khalifah, who was eating a repast in the desert with an
Arab, happened to perceive a hair which had fallen upon

---

* The horse-shoe mc ins the semicircle in which the people sit in
front of the president of :he assembly.

the morsel he was eating, whereon the Khalifah said :—"O Arab! Remove the hair from that piece," but the latter rejoined :—"It is not proper to eat at the table of a man who looks so intently at the morsel one is eating, that he sees one hair upon it." Accordingly he ceased eating and swore an oath that he would never do so at the Khalifah's table.

Verses :

When the host lays out the table of liberality it will be better
To abstain from scrutinizing his guest ;
Who places the food on the table must not
Look stealthily with his eye and count it in his heart.

PLEASANTRY.

In a company the perfections and defects of men were being discussed, when one of those present said :—"Who has not two seeing eyes is but half a man ; who has not a nice wife in his house is half a man ; and who has not travelled is half a man." A blind man who was present in the assembly and had no wife, nor knew how to voyage on the sea, exclaimed :—"My good friend, thou hast done a wonderful thing by thus altogether throwing me out from the circle of mankind, because half a man is required to remove from me the opprobrium of being no man at all."

Verses :

The fellow had so fallen away from mankind,
By his shrunk condition inexperience and coldness,

I

That if men confer a thousand benefits upon him
He will not step out from the limits of no-manhood.

PLEASANTRY.

Bahlûl waited upon Hârûm Rashîd, when one of the wazirs encountered him saying :—" I have good news for thee, O Bahlûl ; the commander of the Faithful has appointed thee to be the officer and Amir over the monkeys and pigs." Bahlûl replied :—" Pay attention to what I say, and obey my commands, for thou art likewise one of my subjects."

Verses :

Thou givest me tidings of my royalty over cows and asses,
The special subject of the king art thou ;
Number my army of bears and pigs,
The first who belongs to this number is thyself.

PLEASANTRY.

A rich man died during the reign of a tyrant. The wazir of the said tyrant asked the son of the deceased what his father had left ? He enumerated the property, goods and chattels, adding that the wazir (may Allah preserve him) had been constituted joint heir with himself. The wazir smiled, ordered the property to be divided in two, one half of which he left for himself, and the other moiety he took away for the Pâdshâh :—

Verses :

A tyrannical wazir does not know
Except the right of the Pâdshâh to the property of an orphan;

He considers it just if he confiscates the whole,
He considers it virtuous if he divides it in twain.

PLEASANTRY.

A Turk, having been asked what he preferred ; the plunder
of to-day, or the paradise of to-morrow, replied :—" My
opinion is, that we should plunder to-day, take all we can,
and go to-morrow into the fire with Pharao."

Verses :

Hast thou learnt, that when a Turk heard of paradise
He asked the preacher if sack and plunder might be there ?
No, quoth he.   Then, said the Turk, that paradise
Bereft of plunder, must be worse than hell.

PLEASANTRY.

A mendicant begged at the door of a house, whereon the
landlord apologised, saying that the people had gone out,
and the beggar rejoined :—" I want a morsel of bread, and
not the people of the house."

Verses :

When a beggar comes to thy door
Make no excuses, give him what thou hast;
Lest he might think ill of thee,
Mention not the people of the house.

PLEASANTRY.

The son of a schoolmaster fell sick and was on the point
of death, whereon he said :—" Bring the *Ghussâl** and wash

---

* This is the name of the professional corpse-washer.

him," and being told that the boy was not yet dead, he continued :—" Never mind, he will die when the washing is finished."

Verses :

Who follows the impulse of his nature and hastens
To do his business before the proper time arrives,
Is like him who eats his supper before the night,
Or him who pulls off his shoes before the water is reached.

PLEASANTRY.

The son of a schoolmaster being told that he was a terrible fool, replied :—" If I were not a fool I would be an illegitimate son."

Verses :

The mother's fault is inherent in her son,
His nature and peculiarities are not the father's;
Only the long ears of the mule bear witness
That his father was not a horse but an ass.

PLEASANTRY.

A schoolmaster having been asked whether he was taller than his brother, replied :—" I am taller, but after the lapse of one year he will be as tall as myself."*

Verses :

As thou hast gained nothing, why askest thou
How the time of such and such a man elapses ;

---

* If for the words *tall* and *taller* in the text, *old* and *older* had occur-red, it would have been more in accordance with the last two lines of the verses which follow.

Thou numberest the years of men and knowest not
That with theirs thy own also pass away.

PLEASANTRY.

A sick man, at the point of death, was visited by a friend
who had a stinking breath, and sitting near his pillow, approached it still more with his head, uttering the *Shehâdat,**
and breathing into his face. The sick man turned his face
away, but his friend only importuned him more and put his
head closer ; whereon the sick man lost his patience and
said :—" Dear fellow, thou wilt not allow me to die cleanly
and pleasantly, but desirest to pollute my death with whatever is most impure and unpleasant."

Verses :

Virtuous men are scarce in this world,
Every chatterer is not to be listened to.
Whose lips exhale the smell of hypocrisy,
His breath is not to be accepted.

PLEASANTRY.

A man was visited by a stranger who began complaining
and said :—" Is it possible that thou knowest me not, and
dost not consider my claims upon thee?" The man was
amazed, and replied :—" I know nothing of what thou

---

* This—literally meaning *testimony*—is the profession of Faith :—
" No God but Allah, Muhammad, apostle of Allah," to utter which is
laudable at all times, but it is also whispered to persons in the agony
of death. This expression is called *Shehâdat*, because in its larger form
it begins with the words *And ashâd*, " *I bear witness.*"

sayest." He continued :—"My father desired to wed thy mother, and if he had married her we would be brothers." The man rejoined :—"By Allah ! This relationship will be the occasion for my becoming thy heir, and thou mine ! "

Verses :

A man of unripe sense fondly imagines that on all
It is incumbent to bestow favours upon him ;
And if his intellect is not ripened in time
He falls into distress, anxiety, trouble, and misery.

PLEASANTRY.

A hunchback having been asked whether he should like if God the Most High were to straighten his back like those of other people, or theirs to become crooked like his own, replied :—" I should like them all to become hunchbacks like myself, so that I might look at them in the same way as they look upon me."

Verses :

It would please thee to see thyself delivered
From a fault wherewith a foe is reproaching thee,
But still pleasanter than this deliverance
To see him afflicted with the same.

PLEASANTRY.

A man said his prayers and then began his supplications, desiring to enter paradise and to be delivered from the fire of hell. An old woman, who happened to be in his rear, and heard him, said :—" O Lord ! Cause me to share in whatever he supplicates for." The man, who had listened, then said :—" O Lord, hang me on a gibbet, and cause me to die of scourging." The hag continued :—" O Lord, pardon me and preserve me from what he asked for." The man then turned to her and said :—" What a wonderfully unpleasant partner this is ! She desires to share with me in all that gives rest and pleasure, but refuses to be my partner in distress and misery."

Verses :

That person is not just, who, when thy desire
Thou obtainest from God, becomes thy partner ;
But who, when fortune turns,
Retraces even his first step.

PLEASANTRY.

A woman lodged against her husband a complaint with the Qâzi, saying :—" He never leaves me alone for a moment, neither in private nor in public, neither when I leaven nor when I bake bread, neither when I am keeping a fast, nor when I am saying my prayers." Her husband rejoined :—" I have married thee for that purpose." The woman continued : —" O Qâzi ! Tell me for a certainty, how many times is he to approach me during a day and night, that I may know and behave correctly." The Qâzi said :—" Ten times."— " I cannot bear it."—" Nine times."—" I cannot bear it."— Haggling in this manner she reduced the number to five, which, however, she was likewise unwilling to agree to. Then the Qâzi exclaimed :—" Woe be to thee, shall this poor fellow not have any share of thee at all ? " Then the woman consented, but the husband said ;—" O Qâzi! Order

her to make some one her security." She continued :—
" Behold, the Qâzi of Musalmâns is my security." The
Qâzi then said :—" O adulteress ! Wishest thou to escape
from him, and throw him upon my hands, that he may
trouble me as much as he troubles thee ? Arise and obey
thy husband."

Verses :

Be the security of no one in matters of lust,
I fear thou wilt be abused, even if thou art 1000 times like
  Joseph ;*
Time and temptation will bring on the fall
Of a chaste man when he is security for a courtezan.

PLEASANTRY.

An old man, who had spent his youth in profligacy and
lost his sexual force, purchased a beautiful slave girl and
dallied with her at the first opportunity; and, although he was
full of lust, his physical ability failed to second his intention.
Accordingly he said to the girl :—" Be kind enough to open
the hand of favour ; arouse this sleeper, and resuscitate this
corpse."

Verses :

The thread of my tool being very weak
Help it by rubbing, O good woman;
Unless thou smoothest the thread with the finger
It cannot be made to enter the eye of the needle.

---

* The abstinence of Joseph towards Pharaoh's wife is meant, which is
narrated also in the Qurân at considerable length.

Although the slave girl did what she had been told, she was unsuccessful, and said the following verses aside from the old man :—

Verses :

The tool of the old man has not reached the destination
But sleeps weak like a corpse,
If thou raisest it by force of the hand,
Which being withdrawn, it falls asleep again.

PLEASANTRY.

A man had a claim of one hundred dirhems against a vagabond, and the Qâzi asked whether he had a witness ? On his giving a negative reply, the Qâzi said :—" Make him swear an oath." The man replied that a vagabond's oath was of no value :—

Verses :

He swears a thousand false oaths every moment
As easily as an Arab eats sour milk in the desert.

The vagabond said :—"O Qâzi of Musalmâns ! If thou believest not my oath, there is in the mosque of our part of the town an *Emâm*,* who is abstemious, veracious, and beneficent. Call him and make him swear an oath instead of me, to set the mind of the fellow at rest."

PLEASANTRY.

An Arab, whose camel had strayed, swore an oath that he would, on finding it, sell it for one dirhem. When he

---

* So called because he is the leader in public affairs.

had again obtained possession of the animal he repented of his oath, but tied a cat to the neck of the camel and shouted: —" Who will buy a camel for one dirhem and a cat for a hundred dirhems? But I do not sell them separately." A man who was there said :—" How cheap would this camel be if it had no collar on the neck ! "

Verses :

If a miser presents thee with a camel, accept it not,
Because contrary to the usage of liberal men,
He will tie a collar of obligations upon its neck
Which will be much heavier than the camel itself.

PLEASANTRY.

A certain physician covered his head with a veil whenever he had occasion to enter the cemetery, and being asked why he did this, he replied :—" Every one whom I pass has received a blow from me, and every one whom I look at, has died from my sherbet."

Verses :

O thou who art unable to cure the sick,
Thy approach is the sign of the coming of death.
In the reign of death the obligation of taking life
Has been removed by thee from the neck of 'Azrâil.*

Verses :

O unskilled physician with scanty customers
Although patients are distressed by thee,

---

* Name of the angel of death, who comes and takes away the soul of a dying person.

By the favour of Allah thou makest glad the heart
Of the corpse-washer, the shroud-seller, and the grave-
digger.

PLEASANTRY.

A philosopher said :—"An unskilled physician is a uni-
versal plague."

Verses :

O thou, who art deficient in medicine
And like a general pestilence to the public,
What wonder is it that they give thee curses
To serve as imprecations against the plague.

PLEASANTRY.

We went out one spring day with a company of acquaintances and friends, to enjoy the air of the fields and obtain
a view of the desert. When we had reached a pleasant
spot, and laid out our banquet of provisions, a dog, which
happened to witness the scene from a distance, approached
us, and one of the persons present taking up a stone offered
it to the dog as if it had been bread. The dog smelled it
and immediately retired, taking no notice whatever of our
invitations to return. The company was surprised, and one
of it said :—"Do you know what this dog says? He says,
these unfortunate wretches are hungry and so avaricious
that they eat stones; then what can I hope to obtain from
their table, and what enjoyment can I expect from their
banquet?"

Verses :

Whether a gentleman spreads his banquet near or far
He forthwith gets a share of pleasure there,

The pleasure of a near poor cat is a stick,
The share of a helpless dog afar is a stone.

PLEASANTRY.

A son having been told that his father would die, whereon he would inherit him, replied :—"I would prefer to see him killed in order to become his heir, and at the same time to receive also the blood-ransom."*

Verses :

The son does not want his father but the property
Which he desires to remain ; and not his father.
The father's death and the inheritance do not satisfy him,
He wants the father to be slain, and also ransom to obtain·

PLEASANTRY.

A beautiful slave girl passed near a man, who then followed her, and she asked :—" Art thou desirous to do to me what my master does ?" He replied in the affirmative, " Yes," whereon she said :—" Then sit down that my owner may first do to thee what he is doing to me."

Versified Pleasantry.

A boy's father had returned from a journey,
He asked every one who passed near the door,
Saying :—" Give me gold and silver, Sir,
For the good news of my father's coming."

---

* A murderer paid ransom according to a fixed scale, to the heir of the man slain by him.

A wide-awake fellow replied :—" O child,
His arrival is not by all approved ;
Thy mother's husband has from his journey come,
Ask thy present from thy mother's womb.''

PLEASANTRY.

Two poets were sitting at a table upon which hot *Pâlûdah**
had been placed. One of them said, this is hotter than the
" boiling hot water" and the "corruption which flows from the
dead bodies of the damned "† which thou wilt drink to-
morrow in hell. The other poet replied :— " Blow one
distich of thy poetry upon it, to relieve thyself and also
others."

Verses :

Of thy cold poetry a single distich,
If written upon the portals of hell,
Would remove the heat of fire from the place
And change the " boiling hot water " to the cold of ice.

PLEASANTRY.

A poet brought to a critic a composition, every distich of
which he had plagiarised from a different collection of poems
and every rhetorical figure from another author. The critic
said :--" For a wonder thou hast brought a line of camels

---

* This word has already been explained in the footnote on p. 98.

† The words above, marked by signs of quotation are only two in
number in Arabic and occur in the Qurân, but in English it is necessary
to use several for each of them, in order to express their meaning
properly.

but if the string were untied, every one of the herd would
rush away in another direction."

Verses :

In the conceit of thy pretension thou hast said
" Compared to my sweet poetry honey is naught."
Thou hast scraped distichs together from every place,
In thy Diwân I preceive nothing besides ;
If each of them were to return to its place
Instead of them only blank paper would remain.

PLEASANTRY.

Farazdaq had written a panegyric on the King of Bosrah,
whose name was Khâled, 'but receiving no commensurate
reward, lampooned him as follows :—

Verses :

I saw the outside of the palace adorned,
I commenced to praise the lord of it,
But my undergarment defiled my nice poetry
With filth, when I began the panegyric.

When these two distichs had been brought to the notice of
Khâled, he sent him one thousand dirhems, with the
message :—" Wash out with these dirhems the meaning thou
hast produced from thy inside, and with which thou hast
defiled the outside."

Verses :

Wonder not if the praised man bestows gifts
Upon his panegyrist although he mixes bad with good.
For his own benefit he bestows gifts, because with them
He washes from the poet's mind the blame attributed to him.

PLEASANTRY.

A poet recited some verses to a critic, and when he had finished, he said :—" I composed this in the privy." The critic replied :—" By Allah ! Thou hast spoken the truth, because these verses exhale the odour of it."

Verses :

Let not a poet say that his verses
Have come out pure from a turbid sea ;
The nostrils of a man of taste are informed
By the breeze, whence they have come.

PLEASANTRY.

A poet paid a visit to a doctor, and said :—" Something has become knotted in my heart which makes me uncomfortable. It makes also my limbs wither, and causes the hairs of my body to stand on end." The physician who was a shrewd man, asked :—" Very likely thou hast not yet recited to any one thy latest verses." The poet replied :— " Just so." The doctor continued :—" Then recite them." He complied, was requested to repeat them, and again to rehearse them for the third time. After he had done so, the doctor said :—" Now arise, for thou art saved. This poetry had become knotted in thy heart, and the dryness of it took effect upon the outside, but, as thou hast relieved thy heart, thou art cured."

Verses :

What verses are these, that if thou askest
All the people will scoff at them,

And if thou recitest them over over the sherbet of a patient
The burning fever ceases, and the cold sets in ?

PLEASANTRY.

A preacher recited in the pulpit some worthless verses,
and boasted of having done so during prayers; but one who
had been present, observed :—"Such paltry verses were
recited during prayers, and what will be the value of the
prayers during which they were recited ?"

Verses :

Thou boastest of having in last night's prayers recited
Verses which excel the compositions of all poets ;
But if these verses had issued from the lower aperture
They would have made thy prayers and ablution invalid.

Verses :

A poetaster recited a poem full of defects,
Remarkable by the absence of the letter *alf ;* *
I said to him, the best artifice would have been
The absence of every letter of the alphabet.

Verses :

Last night he pretented to recite an exordium,
Seeing that it was neither a sea (bahar) of jewels
How could he simply recite it as a sea (bahar)
Since every line of it is in another metre (bahar). †

---

* *Alf* is the name of the first letter of the alphabet.

† The play is on the Arabic word *bahar*, which means a sea, and
also a poetical metre ; but to use another in every line is absurd, and
betrays ignorance of the rules.

Verses :

If thou art not able to recite, sit quiet and cross thy arms,

The product of thy imagination is beyond thy poetical faculty,

How could these qualities bring disgrace upon thy poetry,

Since such defects have not injured the dignity of the prophet.*

---

* The prophet disliked poets; see Qurân, ch. XXVI., v. 224; ch. LII., v. 30; also footnotes on page 132.

K

SEVENTH GARDEN

Account of the rhyming birds of rhetorical nightingales and parrots of the sugar plantation of poetry.

According to the definition of the ancients a poetical composition is the offspring of imagination, acting also upon that of the hearer, no matter whether it be true or not, or convincing to every hearer or not, as for instance, when wine is said to be a molten ruby, or simply a ruby, and honey a bitter or brackish thing vomited by bees. To this definition later scholars have added measure and rhyme as of importance, whilst others consider only these two to be such. Wherefore poetry is a composition according to measure and rhyme; the presence or want of imagination therein, and the truth or absence of truth, being of no account.

Verses :

There is no mistress like words of poetry,
The acme of beauty is not beyond its province,
Patience without it is hard, and consolation difficult,
Especially when a heart is to be conquered ;
It dons an elegant robe of measure
And embroiders its skirts with rhymes,

Adorns them with the anklets of the *redif*,*
On the forehead it adds the mole of imagination,
To the cheek it imparts with *teshbiah*† splendour like the moon,
Bereaving of their senses a hundred persons straying from the way,
It parts the hair asunder by *tajnis*,‡
The mole above divides the plaited curls.
By *tarsi*§ it makes the lips jewel-dropping,
Suspends the precious stones from the musky locks.
By *aihâm*‖ it causes the eyes to twinkle
Throwing confusion into the mental powers.
When it places the ringlets of metaphor on the face
Then truth takes flight and leaves the veil.

The Most High has purified the miraculous Qurân from

---

* The *redif* consists of one or several independent words placed after the rhyme at the end of hemistichs or verses, and these words must be the same in the whole poem, as for instance in the following verse of Th. Moore :—

There shone such truth about *thee*
' I did not dare to doubt *thee*.

† The *teshbiah* is the figure of comparison in which two things are assimilated to each other in one meaning.

‡ The *tajnis* is alliteration, *i.e.* the use of two words similiar in pronunciation but different in meaning.

§ *Tarsi*, literally " to encrust precious stones," means to construct two parallel members of a phrase so that the words of the same measure correspond symmetrically with each other, and even in the final letters.

‖ The *aihâm* or " insinuation " consists in using an expression which has two or more meanings, and the reader is left to conjecture which of them is required.

K 2

the polluting suspicion of its being a poetical composition [saying] that it is *not the discourse of a poet*,* and has lifted the standard of its promulger's eloquence above all mean aspersions, saying :—" *We have not taught him* [i.e. Muhammad] *poetry, nor is it expedient for him.*"† This declaration does not imply that poetry is reprovable by its nature, or that those who write verses are blamable, but it is directed against those who, although possessing no talent, are obstinate and conceited enough to produce poetical compositions. Hence the warning that the prophet (the benediction of Allah be upon him, upon his family and place) is not to be considered a poet. This is a most distinct evidence of the high dignity and exalted position of good poets.

There are various kinds of poems, such as the Qasidah, the Ghazal, the Qal'ah, the Ruba'ayi, &c.,‡ which have been cultivated by various poets, some of whom are believed to have produced verses of every kind, whilst others restricted their efforts only to certain species. Thus for instance, most of the earlier poets wrote Qasidahs, panegyrics, moral poems, &c., whilst some composed Mesnevis, contrary to the later poets, who generally wrote Ghazals, and their number is

---

* Qurân, ch. LXXIX., v. 41.

† Ibidem, ch. XXXVI., v. 69.

‡ For the definitions of these kinds of poems see F. F. Arbuthnot, *Persian Portraits, a sketch of Persian history, literature, and politics,* London, 1887, p. 85 seqq.

boundless, so that to notice all of them would be impossible. Accordingly we shall confine our remarks to a few of the most celebrated :—

Rudaki (the mercy of Allah be upon him) was one of the poets of Transoxiana,* blind from birth, but so sharp and talented that he knew the Qurân by heart at the age of eight years, was able to read it, and also began to compose verses. Having a good voice he became a musician, learnt to perform on the lute, and attained such proficiency that Nasser Ben Ahmad Samani became his patron. It is said that he possessed two hundred slaves, that four hundred camels carried his baggage, and that after his time no other poet enjoyed so much property. His poems amount to one hundred Dufturs (but the responsibility rests upon the informant) and in the Sharh Yamini it is recorded that he wrote one million and three hundred distichs.† The following verses, describing wine, are by him :—

Verses :

Whoever beheld that cornelian wine
Cannot discern it from melted cornelian ;
Both are of one, essence, but in nature
The one is solid, and the other fluid,‡
The one powdered colours the hand, the other tasted mounts
 to the head.

---

* Literally :—" That which is on the other : [Oxus] river,"
ma verâ annahr.

† It would be curious to know how the blind wrote ; perhaps he only dictated.

‡ The text has :—" This is compressed, and is melted. "

Admonitory verses.

Time gave me advice about its turns,
If thou lookest at time, it is all advice ; ·
It said :—Grieve not much for the good days of others
There are many who are longing for thy days.

It is recorded in some chronicles, that Nasser Ben Ahmad, having left Bokhâra, took up his abode at Merv-Shâh-Jehân, and that, when his sojourn there became protracted, his courtiers, missing the attractions of Bokhâra with its palace and gardens, bribed Rudaki with a good round sum to sing verses extolling Bokhâra, to the accompaniment of the lute, on a suitable occasion. Accordingly he did so, one morning after the Pâdshâh had indulged in a libation:—

Verses :

The zephir of the Mûliân river is blowing,
The fragrance of a kind friend is arriving,
The sand, the defects and the roughness of the soil
Appear like embroidered silk to walk upon,
The water of the Jaihûn* with its excellencies
Will again be within our grasp ;
O Bokhâra, be glad, and live long,
The Shâh is coming as a guest to thee ;
The Shâh is the moon and Bokhâra the sky,
The moon is ng into the firmament ;

---

* This is ano, ame for the river Oxus, it is also called Amu-deriah.

The Shâh is a cypress and Bokhâra a garden,
The cypress is approaching the garden.

This performance had such an effect upon the sovereign that he forthwith took horse, with a select company, and travelled one stage. In some chronicles this affair has been attributed to the Sultân Sanjâr and to the Amir Mo'azi, but Allah knows best !

Daqiqi (upon whom be the mercy of Allah) was also one of the early poets, and lived during the sway of the Samânian dynasty. He began the Shâhnâmah, of which he composed about eight thousand verses, and Firdausi completed the work. The following are specimens of his poetry:—

Verses :

He selected a friend of all men, a descendant of fairies,
Wherefore he appeared to my eyes this day like a fairy.
He took an army, and that army-breaking Shâh departed, .
Let him never remain anybody who gave his heart to an
army.

Verses :

I remained here long, I became despicable,
One beloved is considered base if he always remains.
When water remains long in a fruit
It becomes putrid from stagnation.

'Omârah (upon whom be the mercy of Allah) was likewise one of the ancients, and flourished during the time of the Samânians.' He had a pleasant nature and wrote nice verses. The following two distichs are by him.

Verses :

Although the world was for a while silvered by snow
The emerald arrived and took the place of the snow-ball,
The picture gallery of the Kashmirians was in spring
Transmuted into a garden, all coloured with vermilion.

The following verses are also by him :—

Verses :

Be not deceived because the world has exalted thee,
Many a high man was quickly abased by the world ;
This world is a snake, and he who courts it a snake-catcher,
The snake sometimes brings destruction to the snake-
catcher.

It is recorded in the Maqâmât of the Sultân-uttâriqat* Abu
S'aid Abu-l-Khair, that one day a singer recited the following
distich to the Sultân :—

I shall conceal myself in my Ghazal
To kiss thy lip ; recite it nicely.

The Sheikh was pleased, asked who had composed it, and
being told that 'Omârah had written it, said :—" Arise, and
let us pay him a visit." Then he did so with a number of
his disciples.

'Anssari (upon whom be the mercy of Allah) was the
chief poet of his age, and was by Yamin-uddaulah Mahmûd

---

* Chief leader in the *Târiqat*, or road to Sûfi perfection.

Sabagtagîn honoured with the title of Mollah, wherefore
he praised him as follows :—
Verses :
Thou art that Shâh whom, in the east and west,
Jews, Guebres, Christians and Moslems,
All unanimously praise and extol,
O Allah give him a *laudable* end.*

It is said that he wrote numerous Mernevis and panegyrics
on the said Sultân.   One of his poems bears the title of
" Vâmaq and 'Azrâ," of which, however, not a trace remains.

'Asjadi (upon whom be the mercy of Allah) was a native
of Merv, and servant of Yamin-uddaulah Mahmûd Sabagtagîn, whom he congratulated on his conquest of Hindostân,
in a Qassidah, which begins thus :—
Verses :
When the minutely discerning Shâh marched to Sômnât†
He made his exploits the signal for miracles.

He described a melon as follows :—
Verses :
Its colour is that of the topaz, its odour musk, its taste sugar,
It has the hue of brocade and the fragrance of a fresh aloe,
If cut into ten slices each will be a crescent,
If not, it will in its entirety appear like a full moon.

---

* The word is the Sultân's own name, *Mahmûd*, which means *laudable*.
† Name of the celebrated temple in India, destroyed in the 11th cen-
tury by Mahmûd.

Farrakhi (upon whom be the mercy of Allah) also lived during the time of Mahmûd, by whose liberality he accumulated great wealth. He once desired to have a look at Samarqand, but, when he had nearly reached the town, he was robbed by highwaymen of all he possessed; and, after he had entered the town, he did not make himself known, but remained a few days, composed the following verses, and returned again :—

Verses :

I witnessed every one of the delights of Samarqand,
Beheld its gardens, meadows, valley, plain ;
But, as my purse and pocket contained no dirhem,
My heart folded the carpet of pleasure on the surface of
    hope.
From many respectable persons, often in every town,
I heard that there is only one Kawther* but paradises eight.
I saw thousand Kawthers and more than thousand paradises,
But what is the profit, as I am to return with thirsty lips.
When the eye beholds wealth and no money is in the hand,
It is better that the head be cut off than to be in a golden
    dish.

Firdausi (upon whom be the mercy of Allah) was a native of Tûs, whose renown and perfections are well known, and indeed what need to be praised by others has an author who composed the Shâhnâmah ?—It is said that he had been engaged in agriculture, and had met with some injustice, wherefore he

---

* Name of a river in paradise.

proceeded to Ghaznin, the residence of Sultân Mahmûd, to lodge a complaint. When he had arrived, he happened to pass near a garden, where he noticed three men sitting and fully enjoying themselves. He surmised them to belong to the court of the Sultân, wherefore he said to himself:—" I shall go and lay my case before them." When they saw him approach they were displeased, and said :—" This fellow will mar our pleasure, and the best thing to do when he comes will be, to say to him that we are the poets of the Pâdshâh, and do not associate with any other men except poets. We recite three lines rhyming with each other, and associate with every one who gives a fourth line of the same kind. Unless he does so, he must excuse us." When Firdausi had reached them, they informed him of what they had agreed upon ; whereon he said :—" Recite the hemistichs which you have composed." Accordingly

'Anssari said :—The moon is not as brilliant [*rushan*] as thy
    face.

'Asjadi said :—There is no rose in the rose-garden [*gulshan*]
    like thy face.

Farrakhi said :—Thy eyelashes pierce through a cuirass
    [*jushan*].

Lastly Firdausi said :—Like the spear of Giû in the war of
    Pushan.

Then they made inquiries about *Pushan*,* which he fully

---

* This name occurs in the Shâhnâmah and rhymes with the three words given by the poets, who had imagined that there was no fourth of the kind in the language.

satisfied in detail. Being afterwards presented at court, the poet made such a good impression upon the Sultân that he said :—"Thou hast made our assembly like paradise [*Firdausi*]," for which reason the poet henceforth took this word for his *Tukhallus.** Some time afterwards he was appointed to compose a versified king-book [Shâh-nâmah]; and, when he had written one thousand distichs, he brought them to the Sultân, who rewarded him with one thousand dinârs. He completed the work in thirty years, and expected, according to the just mentioned precedent, to receive one dinâr for each distich of it. Envious persons, however, made representations to the Sultân that a poet is not deserving of so high a remuneration, and it was accordingly lowered to the sum of sixty thousand dirhems only. It is said Firdausi was so disgusted, that, happening to be in the bath when the said money was brought, he presented, on going out, one third of the sum to the bathman, as much to an attendant who had often rubbed his body, and the last third to the people who had brought the money. Then he composed a lampoon consisting of about forty distichs, against the Sultân, a few of which are here subjoined ;—

Verses :

If the father of the Shâh had been a Shâh
He would have placed a golden crown on my head,
And if the mother of the Shâh had been a lady
I would wade in silver and gold up to my knees.

---

* The poetical surname assumed is *Tukhallus.*

\

As in his family there was no great man
He could not brook to hear of great men.
A tree the nature whereof is bitter,
If thou plantest it in the garden of paradise
And if thou irrigatest it from the spring of immortality
Or pourest honey and fresh milk on its root ;
It will, after all, manifest its own nature
And produce the bitter fruit due to it.
Entertain no hope from one of impure birth,
Because by washing an Ethiop will not be white,
Who is born of a slave-girl will be useless,
Although he may be the son of a monarch.

After that he concealed himself, and although greatly searched for, could not be found. Khâjah Hasan Maimandi, who occuped the post of wazir, happened some time afterwards, in a hunting party, to recite from the Shâhnâmah some distichs appropriate to an event which had just taken place ; they greatly pleased the Sultân, who asked who had composed them, and, being told that Firdausi had done so, he repented, and ordered sixty thousand dinârs with costly robes of honour, to be·sent to Firdausi, who lived in Tûs. Fate, however, was not propitious, and it is said that, when the royal gifts had been brought into Tûs by one gate, the bier of Firdausi (upon whom be the mercy of Allah) was being carried out by the other. He had left a daughter as his only heiress, to whom the gift was offered, but she refused to accept it, on the plea that she had property enough for her maintenance ; wherefore the money was ultimately spent in the creation of an edifice for the accommodation of travellers.

Verses :

It is blessed to know worth, because, when the vaulted sphere
Bent at last the arrows of events into a bow,
The glory of Mahmûd departed, and time spared
Only the record that he knew not the worth of Firdausi.*

Nasser Khosrû (upon whom be the mercy of Allah) was an excellent poet and great philosopher, but suspected of heresy, infidelity, and even atheism. He composed a *Safar-nâmah* [Travel-book] in which he recorded versified accounts of countries he had visited and conversations of notable men with whom he had become acquainted. The following verses of his occur as a quotation in the book *Zubdutu-l-haqâiq* [Essence of truths] by 'Ayinu-l-qazât, may his secret be sanctified :—

Verses :

All my oppression is from the Bulgarians,
Which I must bear as long as I can,
Nor is it the fault of the Bulgarians ;
I shall tell thee, if thou be willing to hear.
O God ! All this trouble and confusion is from me
But no one dares to reveal it ;
They bring Turks from the Bulgâr
To defile the reputation of men,

---

* The expression *Qausi,* "a bow," is only introduced to make a rhyme with *Firdausi,* and such exigences often make the diction rather awkward, and more so in a translation.

Because from the love of their lips and teeth
It is necessary to bite the lips with the teeth.

Azraqi (upon whom be the mercy of Allah) was skilled in the rules of poetry and the principles of philosophy. It happened that, by an accident, the sexual powers of Sultân Toghânshâh were impaired, and, as the physicians were unable to restore them, Azraqi composed the poem *Alfiah wa Shalfiah* for that purpose. He caused a slave-youth and girl, belonging to the royal household, to be married to each other, and placed them in an apartment in which they were separated from the Pâdshâh only by a grating. Azraqi gave his book to the young couple, and told them to dally with each other according to the pictures represented therein ; he also requested the Pâdshâh to look at them through the grating without their noticing him, and by this spectacle the natural heat of the king became so strengthened that his impotency was removed.

Azraqi's description of wine is as follows :—

Verses :

Cupbearer ! Bring that red wine, the brightness whereof
Makes a tulip-grove appear to be a rose-garden.
If a fairy passes in the night near its rays
She does not remain concealed from the eyes of men ;
It is more fragrant than ambergris, and brighter than a
    ruby,
More shining than a star, more limpid than a running brook.

Mo'azi (upon whom be the mercy of Allah) lived during

reign of Mo'az uddin-wadduniâ Sanjar Ben Melikshâh, and was one of his panegyrists. His name he took from his patron, and but few poets enjoyed emoluments like those which had fallen to his lot. It is said that three poets prospered greatly in three dynasties, and met with much acceptance ; Rudaki during the period of the Samânians, 'Anssari in that of the Mahmûdian and Mo'azi in the Sanjarian dynasty. He was accidently hit by an arrow which the Sultân had shot from his tent, the poet standing outside, and expiring on the spot. The following are specimens of his poetry :—

Verses:

When my love arranged the entangled hyacinth lock of hair
She placed the stamp of envy upon the heart of Chinese
      painters ;
Each heart which bowed from refractoriness to no line
Now bends to that musky streak under her curls ;
I am the slave of that fresh line which resembles
The marks of musk-soiled ant-feet upon the leaf of a wild
      rose.

The following verses are from a Qassidah, composed by him, with figures of speech generally used by Arab poets :—

Verses :

O camel-driver ! Make no halt except in my country
That I may lament over my valleys and ruins,
To fill the valleys with my heart's blood, to make the ruins
      a Jaihûn,*

---

* See footnote on page 134.

To make the soil rose-coloured with the water of my eyes.
The countenance of my beloved is absent from my tent and
hall,
Absent from the meadow is that cypress stature.
The place where that heart-ravisher was with friends in the
garden
Has become the home of wolves, foxes, owls, and of vul-
tures.

'Abdu-l-Wâs'i Jabali (upon whom be the mercy of Allah)
was a talented poet who wrote not only in Persian, but also
in Arabic. The following is a specimen of his poetry :—

Verses :

There is no Belle in the world more inflaming the heart
than thou,
There is in the town no boy, more burning the liver than
thou !
When I have looked at thy blooming lily,
When I have cast a glance upon thy Narcissus full of sleep*
I am sometimes, after meeting thee blooming like a tulip,
Sometimes after separation, drooping my head like a Narcis-
sus.

Adib Sâber (upon whom be the mercy of Allah) was an
eloquent, conspicuous, and agreeable poet, not excelled by
any one in repartee. The superiority of his poems was
generally acknowledged, and Anvari places him above him-

---

* *Narcissus full of sleep* means "a dreamy eye," much admired in the
east.

L

self in a piece in which he enumerates his own perfections,
but terminates with the following distich :—

Verses :

Let all this alone, I am the equal of Khôsrû in poetry,
Am like Sanâyi, although not like Sâber.

The following is one of his pieces :—

Verses :

O thy face is like paradise, thy lips like Salsabil,*
Upon the paradise of thy Salsabil my soul and heart are
    intent ;
My heart feels devotion for thy love, because
It is devotion to find paradise and Salsabil.
How can the planet Venus shine near thy stature ?
How can the sun be beauteous compared to thee ?
Baghdâd is handsome, Egypt attractive, and my eye
Is like the Tigris to Baghdâd and the Nile to Egypt.†
From the burden of thy absence my stature is like a horse-
    shoe,
From the wounds of the hand of love my face is like the
    Nile.‡

The following piece is also by him :—

Verses :

The inkstand, O boy, is an instrument of fortune,
Go and subdue thy unpropitious fortune ;

---

* Name of a fountain in paradise.
† This means that the poet is weeping rivers of tears.
‡ His back is bent like a horse-shoe, and he weeps copiously like the
Nile.

If thou desirest to transmute the inkstand into fortune
Connect the *alf* of it with *ta*, that it may become *lâm*.*

Anvari (upon whom be the mercy of Allah) was an excellent philosopher and perfect orator, who composed beautiful poetry, which indicates his high genius.   His Divân is
celebrated, and one of his compositions, in which he gives
advice to poets, is here inserted :—

Verses :

Last night an amateur said to me :— "Composest thou
    Ghazals ?"
I replied :—"I also washed my hands of panegyrics and
    satires."
He asked :—"How !" and I said :—"That opportunity is
    gone ;
An occasion which is lost, returns no more from non-exis-
    tence ;
I composed Ghazals, panegyrics, satires, all three because
Impelled by greediness, anger, and passion added to them.
A poet is all night in grievous meditation plunged
How to describe lips like sugar, and curls like gems;
Another troubles himself with work all day
Where, from whom, and how, he may gain five dirhems.
As God has, in His mercy, put away into rubbish
These three hungry dogs from my head,

---

* Thus if *a* and *t* be joined the former becomes *l* ; accordingly if دوات
be written دوت *duvât* becomes *dulat*, and *inkstand* is transmuted into
fortune.

L 2

Forbid, O Lord, that I Ghazals, panegyrics and satires com-
pose
Again, since I knowingly did violence to reason.
O Anvari, to boast is not a sign of manliness ;
But, having done so, henceforth restrain thy steps,
Retire to a corner and seek salvation's road ! "

It is said that, when it was brought to the notice of the Sultân of Gûr that Anvari had written a satire against him, he
wrote a letter to the king of Hirât, inviting the poet to come,
in terms of great friendliness, although his intention was to
take revenge, which the king of Hirât shrewdly discovered;
some of the expressions of the said letter being as follows
[in Arabic] :—

Verses :

Let not the duration of my smiles deceive thee,
My exuberance is laughable, but my act deplorable.
Lo, the world says to those who meet her .
Beware, beware of my valour and intrepidity.

Anvari had discovered the purport of these lines by his
sagacity, and, by inducing some persons to intercede for him,
caused the king of Hirât to give up his intention of surren-
dering the poet ; but the Sultân of Gûr again insisted, and
promised to give one thousand sheep, which offer the king
of Hirât communicated to Anvari, telling him that they
must now forsooth part, whereon he replied :—" O Pâdshâh!
Surely a man who is worth a thousand sheep will not be
useless to thee. Allow me to spend the rest of my life in
thy service, and to pour out jewels of praise at thy feet."
The king of Hirât assented, and retained him.

Rashid Watwât (upon whom be the mercy of Allah) was
a poet in Transoxiana and the most eminent of his time.
He composed the *Hadâiq-us-sahr* [gardens of enchantment]
and said in a conversation to one of the wazirs :—
Verses :
Thou art a wazir and I thy panegyrist,
And thou seest my hands empty of gifts ;
Surrender the wazirship to me, and
Praise me, to see my remuneration.
The following verses are also by him :—
My eyes are full of the figure of the Friend,*
My vision is delightful because it contains the Friend,
Nor is it good to separate the vision from the Friend,
He serves me instead of sight, hence he is my sight.
Also :—
Thinking of thee ! Without thee this fleeting world
I abandoned, O Moon ! And thou art not aware !
I washed my hands of all things and lonely sat,
As the storm passed without thee, let it pass again.

'Am'aq (upon whom be the mercy of Allah) also flourished
in Transoxiana, and was the chief poet of his time. One of
his Qassidahs, which is very graceful, begins as follows :—
If there be a speaking ant and a living hair
I am that ant and that hair with life.
My body is like the shadow of a hair, my heart an ant's eye,
Because she with the perfumed hair and ant-waist is absent ;

---

* See footnote on page 19.

If I associate night and day with a hair or an ant
Neither the ant nor the hair will obtain cognizance of me,
I could hide myself in a hair, so lean and weak am I,
If so willed an ant might conceal me in her eye.
I am that ant, which weeping thinned like an hair,
I am that hair which weakness made smaller than an ant.

Sûzeni (upon whom be the mercy of Allah) was born at
Nasf and went ot Bokhâra to pursue his studies, where he
gained a living by enrolling himself as apprentice to a needle
maker, in whose craft he acquired perfection. He chiefly
composed lampoons, and the following verses are from a
Qassidah of his in which he apologises for his frivolities :—

Verses :

How long shall we, by the turning of the glass-coloured
     sphere,
Throw stones upon the glass of the house of devotion.
We make it our buisness to throw stones on the glass
And bring accusations against the glass-coloured sphere.

The following verses are also from one of his Qassidahs :—

I am a thousandfold worse than thou supposest,
No one knows me in this respect as I know myself,
Outwardly I am bad, inwardly worse than bad,
God, however, knows how I am in public and private ;
Satan showed me the way to one small sin
Now I am Satan's guide to a thousand great ones.

The following verses also occur in one of his Qassidahs :—

When thou shootest the arrow of thy charming glance
Make my desolate heart thy target, O *Ghâzi.*[*]
First I began the game of dalliance with thee,
As I have lost my heart, the body I jeopardize,
Since, O friend, thy arrow's wound is soothing,
Either strike me with a glance or rejoice me with a kiss ;
Thou hast a thousand lovers, and I am one more,
Thou wilt not come to me before thou satisfiest them all.

Khâqâni Shirvâni (upon whom be the mercy of Allah)
excelled all the other poets in the peculiar arrangement of
his words, and in his moral compositions, in which, however, his style somewhat resembles that of Hakim Sanâyi.
He boasts of his own genius as follows :

Verses :

I am the first of poets, the banquet of meanings is mine,
'Anssari and Rudaki pick crumbs from my table,
My name is living like a sage's soul because it is fresh,
My greed has become precious like wealth, because it is
     scarce.

Rashid Watwât praises him as follows :—

Verses :

Thou art the sun and moon of the sphere of power
The prime minister on the throne of excellence,

---

[*] Here he compares his mistress to a knight fighting for religion, a
Ghâzi.

Afzaluddin, possessor of virtues, sea of excellence,
Philosopher in religion, breaker of infidelity.

One of his own pieces is as follows :—

Verses :

Cease to grieve for mistresses, O Khâqâni,
Such grief destroys the balance of the mind ;
The face of a beauty is only a mirror,
Bright without, but dark within.

He composed a Mesnevi, called *Juhfatu-l-'Erâqîn* [gift of
the two Erâqs]† which begins as follows :—

Verses :

We are the melancholy spectators
In this green box and clod of earth,‡   .
Whilst this box and clod are in their place
They open the top of the purse of life ;
And these strange objects on the surface of the time,
The clod of the globe and box of the firmament,
Are themselves wonders of magic,
Sometimes ermine, and sometimes sugar-cane.§
There will be a season when time comes to an end

---

* Meaning *Most religious.*

† There are namely two Erâqs, the Arab and the Persian.

‡ The green, or rather blue, vault of the sky, and our globe, as will
appear further on.

§ This is an allusion to the change of seasons, winter and summer ;
the former being represented by the snowy robe of ermine, whilst the
latter is clad in the brilliant green hue of the fields planted with sugar-
cane.

When the deluge of annihilation arrives,
It will be the time when these four bearers*
Lay down the litter of the years and months,
A time when the steeds of the constellations
Throw off their horseshoes and their hoofs also.†

Fakhr Jorjâni (upon whom be the mercy of Allah) was one of the eminent poets of his time. He composed the book *Weis and Râmin,*‡ which has become very scarce in our time, and the following is a specimen from it :—

Verses :
Those conversant with the world cherish the maxim
That literary controversies are easy,
But I do not like the golden basin
In which my antagonist would like to see my blood.
A snake will only beget a snake,
An evil branch will bring forth evil fruit.
Travel is not pleasant, even in health,
Then see what it will be in weakness and disease.
The Narcissus flower is pleasing to the sight
But when tasted it is very bitter.
It is a slighter sin to be unknown among men
Than to speak of what never existed.
A Padshâh may be likened to fire,

---

* The four cardinal points, S., N., E., and W., are meant.
† I am unable to explain this line.
‡ This poem was printed many years ago at Calcutta, in the *Bibliotheca Indica.*

By nature fire is always refractory,
If thou hast the force of the elephant or the lion's nature
Do not be valorous towards burning fire.

Zâhir Fâriâbi (upon whom be the mercy of Allah) was celebrated in .his time. His Divân is well known for elegance, popularity and facility of style. Having obtained favours from the Atabek Abu-Bakar, he one night recited the following piece in the assembly :—

Verses :
O thou for whose wellbeing angels pray,
In this age there is no other chief like thee ;
The scabbard of thy sword said to thy foe
Let the secret of my heart be the ransom for thy head.*

On the above occasion he was presented with one thousand gold dinârs, whereon he recited the following piece :—

Verses :
O Shâh ! By thee the country and religion are in order,
By thy justice the spirit of tyranny and revolt is in agony,
In thy reign the Râfezi and the Sunni both†
Have agreed that Abu-Bakar is in the right.

---

* In the above piece the play'is on the word *ser*, which occurs not less than five times in those four lines, and means head, chief, &c., and the last time " secret," when it is to be pronounced *sirr*; it was of course impossible to render the alliteration into English.

† The names of two well known antagonistic sects.

The following verses in a graceful Mesnevi form are also by
him :—

A learned man from the top of the pulpit announced
That when the hidden abode is revealed*
White beards shall for their sins
Be changed by God to black,
Thus black beards on the day of hope
Will from white beards protection seek.
A red-bearded man of the congregation
Touched his beard on hearing this
And said :—" We are not mentioned in this case,
Count we for nothing in both worlds?"

He acquired celebrity by comparison, and, poets being un-
certain whether he or Anvari was deserving of preference,
one of them said, by way of query :—

Verses :

O thou worthy earth which enhancest the excellence of the
    sky,†
Art thou of blessed aspect and of sun-like countenance ?
People skilled in letters prefer Zâhir's verses
To the poetical compositions of Anvari,
Others, again, contradict these assertions
And continue to wrangle, but who is right ?

---

* By this figure of speech the place and time of the last judgment
are designated.

† Is Zâhir compared to the earth and Anvari to the sky?

Imâm Haruvi replied to the above as follows :—

Verses :

O asker of questions, in these reflections
Thou art not excused if thou seest the truth.
After discerning properly this matter
There is no necessity of spreading explanations ;
One is a miracle the other a scorcery, one a light the other
a lamp,
The one a moon the other a star, the one a sun the other a _
fairy.

Another poet again rejoined as follows :—

Verses :

Every beginner, who thoughtlessly prefers
The verses of Zâhir to the pure diction of Anvari,
Resembles the multitude who could not distinguish
The miracles of Moses from the magic of Sâmeri.*

Nizâmi Ganjavi (upon whom be the mercy of Allah) was
a native of Ganjah. His qualities are more evident than the
sun, and need not be dilated upon ; the gracefulness displayed by him in his *Punj Gunj* was attained by no one,
nor destined to fall to the lot of any human being, although
poets have but little discussed that book. The following
Ghazal is by him :—

Ghazal :

My grief arises altogether from that wheat-hue cheek,
For it all night my sunken cheek is full of blood.

---

* Sâmeri was the maker of the golden calf to be worshipped by the
Jews in the desert, and Moses worked miracles in Egypt. See Qurân,
ch. XX., v. 87.

Her grain of wheat has a moist hyacinth for fruit,
Her smallest ear of corn is the *Virgo* of the firmament ! ! !
I have become heart broken with grief and pale like wheat,
She cares not one straw how Nizâmi fares.

Kamâl Isfahâni (upon whom be the mercy of Allah) has been surnamed the *discerner of meanings* on account of the subtlety he embodied in the significations of his verses, in which he was unequalled by any of the ancient and modern poets ; they, however, excel him in various other qualities.

Salmân Sâveji (upon whom be the mercy of Allah) was an eloquent poet, who wrote with great fluency and employed beautiful metaphors. He wrote imitations of Qassi-dahs composed by celebrated poets, some of which are superior to the originals, whilst others are equal to them. Some of his pecularities of style are more excellent than those of others, and more especially than those of Kamâl Ism'ail, which he repeated in his own poems, but, as he improved them in form and manner, he is not to be blamed.

Verses :

A good signification is [like] a Belle with a pure body,
Dressed [by style] for a while in a robe of different colours,
Her borrowed garment [of style] then becomes her dress of
    honour,
If it be insufficient, more is put on to enhance her beauty.
It is nice to remove the patched woolen cloth [of rude com-
    position],
To robe her in atlas and satin [of elegant style] instead.

He composed two Mesnevi books named *Jamshid* and ·
Khôrshid, upon which he spent so much labour that they
are superior to the *Châsheni* '*Ishq wa Muhabbat* [The banquet
of amorousness and love]. His *Farâq-na-Mah* [Book of
separation] is also an exquisite and graceful poem. His
Ghazals are elegant and pleasing, but the *Châsheni*, being
deficient in these qualities, is not as much appreciated by
men of taste as they are. The following is a specimen of
his composition :—

Verses :

O heart ! How canst thou fill the lap of greediness
With *avarice*, which consists of three hollow letters.*
My friend ! Knock at the door of poverty and content,
Because avarice begets vileness, and content honours ;
If thy foot stumbles, pass on, and mind it not,
Let thy happiness consist in poverty and content.

Muhammad 'Ussâr Tabrizi (upon whom be the mercy of
Allah) wrote the book *Mihr wa Mushtari*, in which he
embodied many graceful artifices, and the following few
amatory distichs are a specimen from it :—

Verses :

Presenting upon the Nasrin rose the nose
As a line perfectly beautiful and elegant,
Created by the hand of destiny like a silver column
Beneath those two arches filled with ambergris ;

---

* This triliteral word is *tom'a* طمع and, as may be seen, each letter of
it contains a cavity.

On the healthy red face of that rose stature
It grew like a nugget of pure silver,
The rose is beautiful but yet undeveloped
Sleeping between the jessamine and the tulip.*

The following verses are also by him :—

Verses :

O 'Ussâr ! Seek not kindness from human nature,
Because a rose will never grow in barren soil.
Faithfulness shuns the senseless face of man
As he from the face of angels flees.
Upon mankind from the sieve of the sky
Fate pours out only the dust of treachery.
For love, he, whose good thou wishest most,
Will every time repay thee with ingratitude.
He whom thou harbourest in thy eyes like tears
Will shed thy blood when he obtains a chance.

Shaikh S'adi Shirâsi (upon whom be the mercy of Allah)
bore the name of Muslih-uddin, and *S'adi* (endued with
felicity) is only a laudatory epithet. He is a model for
writers of Ghazals, and his works command the approbation
of all. A poet had truly said of him :—

Verses :

In poetry three men are poets
After whom no others will appear,

---

* In the above verses the human face is likened to a Nasrin rose, on
which the nose appears to be like a silver column or a nugget of pure
silver.

In description, Qassidah and Ghazal,
Firdausi, Anvari, and S'adi.

Khâjah Hâfez Shirâzi (upon whom be the mercy of Allah)
wrote exquisite poetry, and his Ghazals are superior in
fluency and elegance, but some contain errors in their versi-
fication; and, as no sign of labour appears in them, he was
surnamed *lesânu-l-ghîb*, "tongue of the invisible world" [as
if he had obtained his verses ready made from heaven, without any trouble of his own].

Khâjah Kamâl Khojandi (upon whom be the mercy of
Allah) attained the highest degree of elegance in the gracefulness of words and subtlety of meanings, but his exaggera-
tions often impair the clearness of his diction, so that he
could not reach the elegance of the *Châsheni 'Ishq wa
muhabbat.** Although he followed in many of his figures of
speech, similes, metres, &c., the method and genius of
Hasan Dehlavi, he excelled him in the gracefulness of his
verses; and he, who called him a thief, probably did so on
account of the just mentioned imitation. In a Divân the
following distich occurs on this subject :—

Verses:
No one has caught me at the head of a flaw,†
Hence it appears that I am a good thief.

---

* This book has already been mentioned as the production of Kamâl
Isfahâni.

† This appears to mean that he did not steal verses with flaws in
them, but only good ones.

Some connoisseurs, who enjoyed the society of the Sheikh and of Hâfez, said that the company of the Sheikh was better than his verses, and the verses of Hâfez better than his company.

Amir Khôsrû Dehlavi (upon whom be the mercy of Allah) was a laudable poet, who composed Qassidahs, Ghazals, and Mesnevis, excelling in each. He imitated Khâqâni, and, although he was not equal in Qassidahs, he surpassed him in Amorous Ghazals, which are remarkable, and generally admired. No one composed a better replica to Nizâmi's *Khâmsah* than he; and he wrote also other Mesnevis, all of which are elegant.

Khâjah Hasan Dehlavi (upon whom be the mercy of Allah) chiefly wrote Ghazals, the rhymes of which are strict, and *redifs,** which are strange, in sweet metres. These qualities he selected and followed as the main points of his poetry; and they make it apparently easy at first sight, but difficult to utter, wherefore it has been nicknamed *prohibitively easy.* He was a contemporary of Khôsrû, associated with him, and they alluded to each other in their writings. Thus he said :—

Verses:

Khôsrû accepts with benevolence,
What I, his servant Hasan, say;

---

* The meaning of this word has been explained in footnote on page 131.

My words are not like Khôsrû's,

The words are those which I utter.

Khâjah 'Imâd Faqih (upon whom be the mercy of Allah) was a Sheikh of Kermân, and possessed a monastery ; to all the visitors of which he recited his verses, with the request to correct them ; wherefore it is said that his poetry is the poetry of all the inhabitants of Kermân.

Khojû Kermâni (upon whom be the merch of Allah) was likewise from Kermân. He produced elegant compositions with approved figures of speech, and was surnamed the " bouquet-binder of poets."

Khâjah 'Ussmat-Ullah (upon whom be the mercy of Allah) was a native of Bokhâra and imitated the Ghazels of Khôsrû.

Besâti (upon whom be the mercy of Allah) was from Samarqand. His verses are not without attractions, but from a perusal of them it appears that they are highly deficient in the qualities which must be acquired by education.

Khayâli (upon whom be the mercy of Allah) composed verses, some of which are not void of imagination.* The following is a specimen of his composition :—

Verses :

O thou, of whose grief-arrows the hearts of lovers are the
    targets,

---

* Imagination is *Khayâl,* and endowed with imagination *Khayâli,* which word is the same as the author's name.

People are engaged with thee, but thou art absent from
their midst ;
Sometimes I reside in a monastery, sometimes in a mosk,
Which means that I am in search of thee from house to
house.

Azeri Esferâni (upon whom be the mercy of Allah)* is one
of the poets of Khorâsân. He was much addicted to inco-
herent expressions, and one of his exordiums is as follows :

Verses :

It was night again, my eye flooded the plain of weeping with
water,
The deluge of tears came, made a night·attack upon the
army of sleep.

Kâtebi was born at Nishâpûr, used many expressions
peculiar to himself in a peculiar. manner, and his verses are
not smooth nor uniform.

Shâhi was from Subzvâr ; his poetry is fluent, with chaste
metaphors and very graceful significations.

'*Arifi* was from Hirât, and wrote the *Gôi wa Chûgân*
[cricket ball and bat] of which the following is a specimen,
describing a horse :—

Verses :

When it ran round the globe of the world
It leapt like a ball of the playground through the plain.

---

* This is the last poet to whose name the usual formula (upon whom
be the mercy of Allah) is affixed, and those after him have not been so
honoured.

Whenever it was drowned in perspiration
It gave occasion for a rain mingled with lightning;
Fire escaped from its hoofs,
The whirlwind followed its tail.
Every time it went to battle
It excelled the zephyr in speed,
Descending from a mountain like a torrent,
Crossing the sea like a wind.

*Sâhib Daulati** has honoured our age by his existence;
and although his royal dignity, endowed by nature and education with great qualities of every kind, is more exalted
than to be enhanced by his fame as a good poet, he
has condescended to become one; and it is meet to place
his name at the top of the list of poets. Although he is by
natural talent able to compose both Turkish and Persian
poetry, he is more partial to the first mentioned language, in
which he has written, perhaps, more than ten thousand
Ghazals and nearly three thousand Mesnevi verses which
may be compared to the Mesnevis of Nizâmi in his *Khamsah*,
although no poet of his time wrote better verses. Among
his Persian writings is a very elegant Qassidah, a replica to
one of Khôsrû Dehlavi, the beginning of which is as follows:—

Verses :
The igneous ruby, which adorns the diadem of Khôsrû,
Is but a burning coal for cooking vain fancies in thy head.

---

* His real name was 'Ali Shir, Amir of Hirât.

He wrote the following quatrain to welcome the return of some person from a journey to the Hejâz.*

Verses:

Judge thou, O azure-coloured firmament,
Who of these two had travelled more gracefully,
Thy world-illuminating sun from the east,
Or the moon of the world to me, from the west.

He wrote in a letter :—

Verses :

This epistle is not the offspring of my grief
But of internal tranquility produced by melancholy ;
It pacifies my warm heart and cold breath,
Meaning that news from the moon of the world is around me.

To the above letter he added :—

Verses :

When I am present I speak and gossip about thee,
When I travel I seek and search for thee ;
When thou art present I am face to face with thee,
In thy absence I turn my heart to thee.

---

* The journey to the Hejâz means a pilgrimage to Mekkah.

EIGHTH GARDEN

*Some stories about dumb animals, which wise and intelligent
men have recorded in the manner of parables to make
them acceptable by their strangeness and
scarcity, as well as useful and
instructive.*

Verses :
Hast thou not seen how a wise man with ṣugar
Makes a bitter medicine sweet ;
By that device from the body of the patient
To remove a long disease and suffering.

STORY.

A fox having cultivated the acquaintance and courted
the friendship of a wolf, they proceeded to a garden where
they halted ; and, seeing that it was surrounded by a hedge
full of thorns, they walked round till they discovered a gap,
wide enough for the fox but narrow for the wolf, so that the
former passed in easily, but the latter with difficulty. They
saw plenty of grapes, and found a variety of fruit. Reynard
being intelligent, considered how he might best be able to
get out again, while the wolf ate as much as he was able.

When the gardener perceived the two intruders, he snatched up a stick to drive them out, and the fox, whose body was slender, succeeded in quickly making his escape, whilst the wolf with his big belly stuck fast, so that the gardener reached him and belaboured him to such a degree that his skin was torn, his wool plucked out, and he escaped more dead than alive from the narrow gap.

Verses:

Boast not of thy gold, O gentleman,
Because at last thou wilt suffer defeat ;
Thy abundant wealth and comfort have fattened thee,
Consider in what manner thou wilt depart.

STORY.

A scorpion, ready to inflict injury with his poisonous sting like an arrow in a quiver, was on a journey ; and, having suddenly arrived near a water, but being unable to cross it and unwilling to retrace his steps, was much perplexed. A tortoise, who noticed the difficulty, took pity upon him, mounted him on his own back, and began swimming to the opposite shore. Suddenly, however, he heard a sound, as if the scorpion had struck his back with something, and, on asking what it was, received the answer : — " This is the sound of my sting upon thy back ; although I know it can · make no impression upon it, I cannot abandon my habit," as a poet says :—

Verses :

The sting of the scorpion is not for inflicting pain
But it is the necessity of his nature to do this.

The tortoise then said to himself :— " I can .do nothing better than to deliver this wicked fellow from his ill-humour, and so prevent him from injuring kind people," whereon he dived, and the scorpion was taken off by the waves as if he had never existed.

Verses :

A companion who in this world of trouble
Is every moment brewing mischief
Is best drowned in the waves of annihilation
To deliver the people from his ill-nature.

STORY.

A mouse dwelt several years in the shop of a grocer, pilfering his dry confectionery and his moist fruits with impunity, because the grocer failed to take measures for putting a stop to his depredations, till one day, according to the saying :—

Verses :

When the belly of a vile fellow is full
He gets bold to commit a thousand tricks.

The greediness of the mouse culminated in his gnawing through the grocer's money bag, abstracting all the gold and silver coins it contained, and concealing them in his hole. Having occasion to take some money, the grocer one day put his hand into the bag, but found it empty like the purse of beggars or the stomach of hungry men. He knew that the mouse had done this, and watched him from an ambush like a cat. He succeeded in catching the mouse whereon he tied a long string to one of his legs, and allowed the mouse to skip, which then at once ran into the hole. Having ascertained the depth by means of the string, and again secured the mouse, the grocer dug up the hole, in which he found silver and gold coins as in the shop of a banker, dinârs and dirhems all mixed together. He took possession of his money and surrendered the mouse to a cat to be punished for his ingratitude.

Verses :

If the greedy people of the world suffer confusion
The glad heart of a contented man is free of it.
In the comfort of content all is tranquility,
In greediness there is no joy, but an aching head.

STORY.

A fox took his position upon the highway, looking right and left to reconnoitre the vicinity, and perceived something dark. After this black object had come nearer, he found it to be a rapacious wolf, walking in close proximity with a big dog, like two intimate friends and harmonious companions, apprehending no treachery nor hostility from each other. The fox went forward, respectfully saluted them, and addressed them as follows :—" Praise be to Allah that the chronic pain has changed to new love, and the old enmity has been transmuted into new friendship ! But I am desirous to know the reason of your reconciliation, and the occasion of your mutual confidence." The dog replied :— " My confidence arises from the enmity of the shepherd, whose enmity towards the wolf stands in no need of explanation, but mine towards him arises from the circumstance that this wolf, the pleasure of whose company I to-day enjoy, ·had attacked the flock and taken away a lamb, whereon I ran after him according to my usual custom, to recover the said lamb from him, and that when I returned, the shepherd chastised me by taking up his stick and beating me without any reason ; therefore I likewise severed my friendly connection with him, and joined my former enemy."

Verses :

Become a friend of thy foe, in such a way
That he will never scratch thy hide with the sword of enmity.
Do not be so inimical towards thy friend,
That in order to injure thee he makes friendship with his foe.

STORY.

One said to a fox :—" Wilt thou take a hundred dirhems, and carry a message to the dogs ?" and he replied :—" By Allah ! Although the reward is abundant, but this affair is fraught with danger to life."

Verses :

To hope for liberality from a base fellow,
Is to surrender a ship to a stormy sea.
To humble oneself to a foe, for the sake of pomp and money
Is to throw oneself into a vortex of danger to life.

STORY.

A camel, browsing in the desert, devoured its thistles and brambles. It reached a thorny bush which was entangled

like the ringlets of a Belle, and blooming like the countenance of a fair maiden. Accordingly he stretched forth the
neck of greediness to have a bite, but, perceiving a viper
coiled up in the bush, his appetite vanished and he retreated.
The thorny bush imagined that the abstinence of the camel
was the result of fear from the sharp teeth of the thorn, but the
camel understood it and said :—" My apprehension resulted
from this hidden guest, not from the known host, and I feared
the sting of the serpent, not the wounds from the thorns ;
had it not been for the guest, the host would have been
forthwith devoured by me."

Verses :

If a noble fellow dreads a miser, it is not strange,
He fears the wicked soul, not his wool and bones.
Who places his foot on hot ashes
Ought to dread the fire concealed under them.

STORY.

A hungry dog, which had reached the gate of a town in
search of food and had taken up a position near it, saw a
round loaf of bread rolling out from the town towards the
desert, and following it he shouted :—" O food of body and
food of soul ; O wish of my heart and peace of my life, what
may be thy intention and where art thou hastening ?" The
loaf replied :—" I am acquainted with some notorious wolves
and tigers, to whom I intend to pay a visit." The dog continued :—" Do not attempt to frighten me, because if thou
enterest the jaws of a crocodile, or the throat of a lion and
tiger, I shall follow thee and not leave thee."

Verses :

I am he who will never in all his life
Cease to long for thee ;
If thou travellest round the whole world,
I shall always seek thee.

Verses :

Those whose soul is kept alive by bread only
Enrol themselves in service for two loaves to gain bread.
Although some persons slap them a hundred times
They run like a hungry dog after the loaf.

STORY.

A crab, having been asked why he walked in a crooked
manner like deformed creatures, replied :—" I take my cue
from the serpent, which by proceeding in a straight line is
always hit on the head by the stone of adversity, and gets its
tail cut off by the strokes of tyranny."

Verses :

Wherever a fairy appears in her own form,
She is embraced and closely hugged like life ;
Wherever she appears in a straight form like a snake
Hard-hearted people strike her from a distance with sticks
    and stones.*

STORY.

A frog, having been separated from his spouse, was sitting
alone in depressed spirits near the bank of a river, and
looked in every direction, when suddenly :—

---

* This is no doubt an allusion to the superstition that a beautiful
serpent is a fairy. She is slain because she appears in a dangerous form.

Verses :

He beheld a fish in the water
Quickly going like the running brook,
With fins like scissors in the liquid silver,
Cutting in twain the atlas of the water surface,
Inclined to skip from right to left,
Or like the bright crescent, now growing, now on the wane.

When the frog caught sight of him, he desired to become the companion of the fish, to whom he narrated his bereavement and expressed his desire for friendship. The fish replied :—"Congeniality is required in companionship, without which it is unsuitable. What harmony is there between me and thee ? I dwell in the depth of the river and thou on the bank of it ; my mouth is dumb, and thy tongue is full of chatter ; thy form is so ugly that no one is willing to associate with thee, whereas my beauteous aspect has become an occasion for the greatest danger and fear ·to me, because any one, whose vision is rejoiced by a glance at my beauty, is anxious for union with me. The fowls of heaven are dazed by their love for me, and the wild animals of the desert are plunged in amorous melancholy for me, whilst fishermen are now searching for me with a thousand eyes like a net,* and now bent like a bow under the weight of desire to see me.' After saying this, the fish went to the bottom of the river, and left the frog on the bank in solitude.

Verses :

Associate with him who is congenial to thee,
The connecting link for harmony is congeniality ;

---

* Here the meshes of the net are likened to so many eyes.

If a wise man contemplates our temperaments
He sees some unite like milk and sugar, some repugnant
like water and oil.

STORY.

A dove, having been asked why she is able to produce
only two young ones, and not several like a hen, answered ;
—"A young pigeon is fed from the mother's and father's
stomach, whereas the chicken of a house-fowl frequents
every dunghill and every road. One stomach cannot feed
more than one young one, but half a dunghill a thousand
chickens."

Verses :

If thou wishest to have abundant food
Keep no numerous family in thy house,
Since thou knowest that in this narrow abode
Allowable food is not very abundant.

STORY.

A sparrow left his ancestral home, and took up his abode
in the chink of a stork's nest. Being asked why he, whose
body was so despicable, had become the neighbour of so
great a bird, and why he considered himself the equal of the
stork in the locality and habitation, he replied :—" I know
all that, but am not able to act according to my wishes. In
my neighbourhood there is a snake, which, whenever I beget
young ones, and feed them with my heart's blood, invades
my house, and devours them. I have fled, and taken protection under this powerful stork, who, I hope, will this year

devour the snake with all his brood, in the same manner as the snake annually devoured mine."

Verses:

When the fox dwells in the desert of lions,
He is secure from the claws and injury of the wolf.
He is secure from the tyranny of the small,
Who takes up his abode in the vicinity of the great.

STORY.

A dog having been asked why no beggar could pass round any house where he happened to be, replied :—" I am far from being greedy, and well known for my contentment. I am satisfied with the crumbs of the table, and with the bones of roast meat, whereas a mendicant is covetous and pretends to be hungry although his bag may be full of bread. His tongue is pleading for a night's repast, whilst he carries two days' provisions on his back, and the staff of mendicancy in his hand. Contentment is far from greediness, and one who is satisfied despises it."

Verses :

That heart in which noble content has taken root,
Abstains from whatever smacks of greediness.
Wherever contentment has laid out its wares
The bazâr of greed and covetousness is broken.

STORY.

The whelp of a fox asked his mother to teach him a trick, how to elude the pursuit of a dog and to escape. The old fox replied :—" Although there are plenty of tricks, the best of them is to sit in thy lair so that neither he may see thee, nor thou him."

Verses :

When a base fellow becomes thy foe, it is not wise
To concoct stratagems for carrying on enmity.
A thousand tricks may be devised, but the best is
Neither to make peace, nor to wage war, with him.

STORY.

A red wasp assaulted a bee to devour it, when the bee said, weeping :—" Considering that there is plenty of sweetness and honey, of what importance am I, that thou shouldst leave it and covet me ? " The wasp replied :—" If this be sweetness thou art the mine of it, and if that be honey, thou art the fountain of it."

Verses :

Blessed is the man of truth who with salutations
Turns his face and seeks the banquet of *union*.*
As the root appears concealed beneath the branch,
He abandons the branch, and goes to the root.

STORY.

An ant was seen, girding the loins of exertion, and dragging a locust ten times his own weight. Some one said :—" Look at this ant, how it pulls such a heavy load in spite of its weakness ? " The ant, hearing these words, smiled and said :—" Men have carried loads by the force of

---

* Union, as has already been observed is the seventh stage in the journey to perfection.

courage, and the arm of self-reliance, not by physical strength and health of constitution."

Verses:

A burden repugnant to heaven and earth to bear
Can scarcely be carried with the aid of body and soul,
Strengthen thy courage by the aid of travellers in the path
    of love,*
Because that load may be carried by the strength of courage.

STORY.

A camel was grazing in the plain and trailing his bridle on the ground. A mouse, seeing the animal without a master, was impelled by greediness to take hold of the bridle, and to start in the direction of his home, followed by the camel; which, being obedient by nature and training, offered no resistance. When they arrived at the home, which was a small hole, the camel said :—" Thou hast attempted an impossible thing; thy house is so small and my body so large. Thy house cannot be enlarged nor my stature diminished; then how can we associate and live with each other ? "

Verses:

How travellest thou the way to death as I see thee ?
With a camel-load of greediness and avarice on thy back ;
Lighten thy burden somewhat, because
The grave has no room to contain it.

STORY.

When a sheep leapt out from the river, her tail happened

---

* The mystic love of the Sûfi doctrines is meant here.

N

to be lifted up, and a woolcarder said laughing :—" I have seen thy *pudenda* !" She turned her head and replied :— " O wretch ! I have for years seen thee stark naked,* but never laughed ! "

Verses :

When a wretch, notorious for a thousand faults
Day and night patent to all the world,
Perceives a small blemish in a noble fellow,
He breathes reproach and execration,
He forthwith blames the faults of him,
Who never defiles his tongue by mentioning his.

STORY.

A cow was the leader of the herd, and celebrated in it for the strength of her horns, because, whenever a wolf approached it, she warded off the attack from it by means of them. All of a sudden, however, a calamity befell this cow so that her horns were injured, and, whenever after that a wolf hove in sight, she took refuge among the other cows. Being asked for the reason, she replied :—

Verses :

From the day when my horns became useless,
My bravery forthwith took leave of me ;
It is an old proverb, that on the day of battle
The stroke comes from the sword, the ambition from the man.

---

* Woolcarders wear no clothes when they are at work, on account of the heat, and because it would be troublesome to clean them afterwards from the fibres.

STORY.

A camel and a donkey happened to travel together, and, on arriving at the bank of a river, the camel entered first. When the camel had reached the middle of the river, the water touched only his belly; whereon he called the donkey to follow him, but the latter replied :—" That is true enough, there is however, a difference between bellies and bellies ; when the water only touches thine, it will overflow mine."

Verses :

O brother ! No one knows thee better than thyself,
Do not exalt thyself a hair's breadth above thy station ;
If a fool exalts thee above what is due to thee,
Know thy own value, and overstep it not.

STORY.

A peacock and a crow, who had met in the area of a garden, were expatiating on their mutual faults and perfections. The peacock said to the crow :—" These red shoes on thy feet would harmonise with my gold-embroidered atlas and variegated brocade ;* we no doubt committed a mistake in putting on our shoes at the time when we emerged from the dark night of non-existence into the bright day of being ; I put on thy shrivelled black shoes, and thou mine of tanned leather, because the rest of thy dress does not harmonise with thy shoes, it is most likely that this exchange has taken place at the said drowsy times." A tortoise of the

---

* According to Eastern opinion a peacock is ashamed of his feet, which are ugly in comparison to his brilliant plumage, and therefore he never looks at them.

vicinity who had been observing them, and heard their conversation, lifted up his head and said : — " O my beloved
companions and discerning friends, leave off useless disputes
and idle talk, God the Most High has not given all things
to one individual, and not granted the fulfilment of all
wishes to one person. He endowed no one with a pecu-
liarity the like of which He has not given also to others, or
bestowed a gift the like of which He has not granted also
to others. Let therefore every one be glad with what has
fallen to his share."

Verses :

To bear envy towards others is not wise,
Wherefore take care not to be unwise.
To be covetous or envious is a source of malady,
Cut off therefore covetousness and thou wilt not be sick.

STORY.

A fox having been grasped by the claws of a hyena who
fixed the teeth of greediness upon him, the fox exclaimed
lamenting :—" O lion of the plain of force, and O tiger of
the top of exaltation, have mercy upon my weakness. I am
but a lump of wool and of bones, release thy grasp of me.
Of what profit will it be to torment and to devour me ? "
and, when these words produced no effect whatever, he continued :—" Remember the obligation under which thou art
towards me, because thou hast expressed a desire for copu-
lation with me. I consented and had several times consecu-
tively sexual connection with thee." When the hyena heard
this base insinuation, he became incensed with wrath,

opened his mouth and shouted :—"What foolish words are these ? When and where had this event taken place ?" As soon however as the hyena opened his mouth [relaxing his grasp] the fox escaped :—

Verses :

If sweet words will not save thee from the foe,
Revile him with thy tongue.
If the house-lock will not open with gentleness,
Then break it with a stone.

STORY.

A jackal having taken a cock by surprise during his morning nap, he said lamenting :—"I am the companion of the wakeful and the Muezzin,* of those who spend the night in prayer ! Kill me not, and shed not my blood with the sword of oppression :—

Verses :

Why quarrelest thou without reason,
And desirest to shed my guiltless blood ?
The jackal replied :—"In my wish to slay thee, I am not so obstinate as not to refrain therefrom by any means. In this matter I leave thee the choice to tell me, whether I am to take thy life with one blow, or to consume thee gradually, morsel after morsel ? "

Verses :

Deliberate well and abandon not thy common sense,

---

* The *Muezzin* is the sacristan of the mosque, who regularly shouts from the top of it the call to prayers at stated times.

If thou be wicked, that confusion and wickedness will over-
take thee ;
Do not think thou wilt be saved by supplication,
If thou escape from bad thou wilt fall into worse.

———◆———

It was the wish of the author's heart, and the intention of
his mind, not to terminate this book so soon, and not to
give rest to the pen in jotting down its contents ; but
although the mirror of the speaker's nature was not obscured
by the rust of tediousness, the speculum of his hearer's inclination has not cheerfully received the polish intended for
him by the furbisher ;* therefore the work is cut short
here :—

Verses :

Spread out, O Jâmi, the carpet of eloquence,
Because there exists not a more beautiful carpet ;
But sit quiet and restrain thy breath,
When the mind feels no inclination ;
Nor is the inclination of the mind enough
If the hearer feels no pleasure.
All the accounts of poems and poets recorded in this treatise
are the offspring of the author's own labour :—

Verses :

Whenever Jâmi produced a literary composition,
He abstained from borrowing the sayings of any one.

---

* From the above remark it would appear that the son of Jâmi was
but an indifferent.pupil, taking very little or no interest in this literary
banquet prepared for his instruction.

He, whose shop is full of wares produced by himself,
Stands in no need of hawking the wares of others.

It is hoped that the noble disposition of readers will induce them to pass over any defects they may meet with, to cover them with the skirts of pardon, and not to indulge in ridicule but rather in leniency.

Verses :

When thou seest a blemish in a friend,
It will be better not to reveal it to strangers.
Because, according to the principles of those who look to
the end,
It is better to conceal faults than search for them.

Verses on the date and termination of the book :—

The trotting and ambling of the pen in this book,
In which Jâmi has tried his talent,
Was finished when the years of the Hegira
Would be nine hundred if eight were added to them.*

The petition to Allah the glorious and bountiful is for great success; but felicity consists in modesty. Benediction and peace to Muhammud, to his exalted family and to his noble companions.

---

* Accordingly the book was finished A. H. 892 which began on the 28th December, 1486.

END.

ERRATA.

Page 3, *for* Jûmi *read* Jâmi.

55, *for* Medinah *read* Madinah.